More Praise for

RIPE

"Etter's exquisite prose powers the book. . . . [She] expertly diverts the novel from neat or didactic tropes . . . [and] accomplishes what we seek in fiction: a deeply human connection."

—*The New York Times Book Review*

"A gut-wrenching story . . . a cutthroat satire."

—*Marie Claire*

"A novel of appetites where hunger is never sated and where consumption fuels the necessity to consume, and thus labor (however cruelly) more."

—*Los Angeles Review of Books*

"A fresh voice, Etter, winner of the Shirley Jackson Award for Best Novel for *The Book of X*, will undoubtedly cement her place in the literary scene with this one."

—Zibby Owens, *Good Morning America*

"This novel is a master class in creating tension. . . . Reminds us that the apocalypse is now. Dystopia is here."

—Roxane Gay

"Etter opens *Ripe* with an onslaught of visceral imagery that stays at a fever pitch all the way through. . . . Taking in Etter's explosive, often grotesque prose in one sitting isn't for the faint of heart. In a weird way, reading *Ripe* feels like being hit over the head with a cast-iron frying pan, then willingly going back for more."

—*San Francisco Chronicle*

"A poignantly tragic, absurdist view of the 'late-capitalist hellscape' that is grind culture . . . [A] glorious sucker punch of a second novel . . . A razor-sharp commentary on the relentlessness of tech culture and millennial striver conditioning . . . *Ripe*, as it wades through Cassie's struggles with clinical depression, could feel dauntingly heavy in different hands, but with Etter's artfully deft and empathetic prose, it's something of a dark adventure."

—*Shondaland*

"At once grim and playful, *Ripe* succeeds where other dystopian novels sometimes fail, by emphasizing the personal and particular agony of a single frazzled rat in the capitalist maze."

—*The Philadelphia Inquirer*

"An explosive narrative of a woman coming undone as the world burns . . . A scathing look at corporate greed and its many dire consequences . . . deeply felt and cathartic."

—*Publishers Weekly* (starred review)

"*Ripe* begins with an evisceration of contemporary San Francisco, laid to waste by the tech industry . . . surreal."

—*Bustle*

"Etter tells this gothic tale of twenty-first-century anomie, isolation, and despair in potent, fast-paced passages that are rich with fairy-tale-esque drama and sharp with parable-esque restraint. . . . Cathartic, addictive, delicious."

—*Chicago Review of Books*

"One of the best novels of the year . . . Etter is proving to be one of the most talented novelists of her generation."

—*The Colorado Sun*

"[An] astonishing tour de force . . . Masterfully juxtaposing 'wild amounts of wealth' with 'extreme poverty and displacement,' Etter examines deep inequities in an image-obsessed, capitalist society. Her biting social commentary layers horror with dark comedy, using vivid imagery and striking language to great effect."

—*Booklist* (starred review)

"HOLY SHIT, this book wrecked me!"

—Samantha Irby, *New York Times* bestselling author of *Quietly Hostile*

"A lurid, tense, and compelling novel . . . Etter builds a lush and decaying landscape around a woman with an impossible affliction. . . . Presenting a cross between the cruel relationships in Mona Awad's *Bunny*, the painful work conditions in Raven Leilani's *Luster*, and the unethical tech-industry practices in Anna Wiener's *Uncanny Valley*, this novel reveals seemingly ordinary terrors. . . . The violence and intensity of Etter's style (as well as its calculated silences and pauses) produce a horror that lingers long after the story has ended."

—*Kirkus Reviews* (starred review)

"A tremendous story . . . Etter treads a fine line between gothic horror and dystopian fiction, snaring Cassie somewhere between our own lived reality and an uncanny, colorless future that is closer than it may seem. . . . Etter is at her best when carving firm lines around this anguish, a relentless haunting that articulates the pure horror of having a body and licensing others to own it."

—*The Sewanee Review*

"A nightmarish depiction of the life of a Silicon Valley worker."

—*The London Magazine*

"[*Ripe*] manages to skewer workplace politics and the vacuousness of modern existence in a way that makes it feel like a fresh subject. . . . Etter captures the cruel facts of San Francisco well: the dystopia that that Eden-like setting has turned into."

—*LitHub*

"Sarah Rose Etter is electric on everything from tech culture's toxic absurdities to bone-deep loneliness to the science of black holes. *Ripe* is a harrowing and mordantly hilarious send-up of the horrors of late-stage capitalism and a potent meditation on the search for meaning in a broken world."

—Laura van den Berg, author of *The Third Hotel*

"Sarah Rose Etter's *Ripe* has the most exquisitely described dread I've read in ages. I couldn't put this book down. Totally haunting and propulsive."

—Halle Butler, author of *The New Me*

"*Ripe* is a triumph—blade-sharp and unflinching. It walks a darkly gorgeous tightrope between the bitter and beautiful with skill that takes your breath away."

—Sophie Mackintosh, author of *The Water Cure*

"*Ripe* is enveloping, a bleakly funny surrealist/realist tale of everyday corruption and panic, and what to do when the void winks at you."

—Elisa Gabbert, author of
The Unreality of Memory

"Freaky and fresh, *Ripe* is a brilliant creature of a book. It is visceral and alive, pumping with blood and juice. A beautiful tangle of wit and tenderness."

—Ella Baxter, author of *New Animal*

Also by Sarah Rose Etter

The Book of X

Tongue Party

RIPE

A Novel

Sarah Rose Etter

SCRIBNER

New York London Toronto Sydney New Delhi

Scribner
An Imprint of Simon & Schuster, LLC
1230 Avenue of the Americas
New York, NY 10020

First Scribner trade paperback edition March 2024

SCRIBNER and design are trademarks of Simon & Schuster, LLC

Simon & Schuster: Celebrating 100 Years of Publishing in 2024

For information about special discounts for bulk purchases, please contact Simon & Schuster Special Sales at 1-866-506-1949 or business@simonandschuster.com.

The Simon & Schuster Speakers Bureau can bring authors to your live event. For more information or to book an event, contact the Simon & Schuster Speakers Bureau at 1-866-248-3049 or visit our website at www.simonspeakers.com.

Interior design by Davina Mock-Maniscalco

Manufactured in the United States of America

10 9 8 7 6 5 4 3 2 1

Library of Congress Control Number: 2022056358

ISBN 978-1-6680-1163-8
ISBN 978-1-6680-1164-5 (pbk)
ISBN 978-1-6680-1165-2 (ebook)

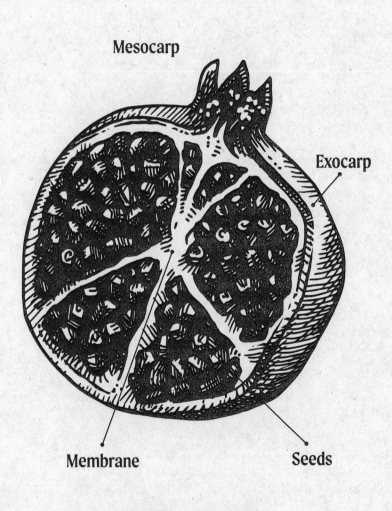

Fig. 1 Pomegranate

exocarp

/ˈeksōˈkärp/

noun

1. the outermost layer of a ripened ovary or fruit, such as the skin of a peach or pomegranate.

A man shouldn't be seen like that, all lit up. A horror that sharp stays with you. It's a knife lodged in the heart. A Tuesday, on the train, in the evening, after work. The train smells of: humans and ruin, bad breath, old sweat, rotten fruit. Through the dirty window, San Francisco in winter: cold sunset over glinting water, dark hills dusted with lights, the black silhouettes of palm fronds clawing at the fading pastel sky.

The train is full of Believers. I'm not one of them. The Believers have wan skin and glassy eyes. They wear: wind jackets with tech logos, raw denim, canvas sneakers, sustainable ballet flats. Their white plastic earbuds override the sound of real life, their faces buried in their screens. They do not speak or make eye contact. They aren't really here. The train is full of husks.

I act like one of them. Slow, sad music plays through my earbuds. The song makes the commute feel like a movie. With each flash of scenery, the train carries me farther away from the office. Each day here presses the life out of me. On the way home, I am silent, flat, pulped.

The black hole hovers above the empty seat to my left. A dark heat emanates from its center. A metallic smell overtakes me, the scent of outer space. No one else can see the black hole. It is mine and mine alone. It always has been.

"Ma'am, I need a dollar," a voice calls over my music.

A man stands in the aisle: faded brown suit, too old to blend in here, his dark eyes bloodshot from age or drink.

"I don't have any cash," I say.

"Nothing? Come on."

The black hole expands and rotates clockwise.

"I'm really sorry."

"Man, fuck you," he mutters, moving on to the next husk.

As the train reaches my stop, I slide my earbuds out and into their case. I weave through the crowd on the platform: mothers pushing strollers, Believers carrying hoverboards under their arms, teenagers cursing, the blind man playing a battered violin, the melancholy notes of the strings vibrating through the belly of the station. The black hole moves alongside me, above their heads.

Outside, I walk a few blocks through the heart of the city: vendors selling food and flowers, performers strumming old guitars with white buckets at their feet, women selling silver jewelry glinting beneath the streetlights. Then I see him.

It starts with a small crowd on the sidewalk. A fire truck and a few police cars are parked haphazardly on the street, blue and red lights flashing.

"Sir, please think this through," a policeman says above the din of the crowd. "You don't need to do this."

Suddenly, an orange flickering shoots above our heads. At first, I think it is a bonfire, but a howl rips through the air and the bodies part. A tall fire blazes, and inside the flames, I make out the shape of a man waving his arms. He opens his mouth in a silent scream.

The firemen turn their extinguishers on him, blanketing his smoldering body in synthetic snow, as the pyre of him collapses on the sidewalk. The wretched scent of charred skin and hair threads through the air.

I can't take another second. I turn away.

The walk to my apartment is a silent hallucination. I imagine the unbearable aftermath on a terrible loop: his seared skin sliding off, exposing the raw red flesh beneath.

The pastel row homes of my neighborhood are gray in the dark. In the entryways of closed stores, people without homes have set up their small, temporary camps for the night. The black hole rises up into the sky before me, a dark star.

Numb and trembling, I pull my phone from my pocket and tap the screen. It's late across the country, but I know he will answer.

"Hey, sweetie."

"Hey, Dad."

"Listen, it's too late to call like this. You know we're sleeping already. You almost woke your mother up. Everything okay?"

The man on fire is caught in my throat. The whole scene lives there, inside my neck, smoldering. I taste smoke.

"It's going okay," I choke out. "Just missed you."

"Miss you, too. Love you."

"Love you, too."

He hangs up and the loneliness in my chest overtakes me for a moment. I reach the front of my building, a cakelike yellow home converted into apartment units. The man who lives on the sidewalk beneath my window is sleeping.

Upstairs in my tiny apartment, I pull a small bag of cocaine from the freezer and cut out a line, then suck the powder up my nostrils. The drugs lace into my blood. I lean back on my cheap blue sofa and stare at the white ceiling. For a moment, just a moment, the man on fire is gone and there is nothing in my mind at all. For a moment, I am cold, still, a cadaver on a silver autopsy table.

But when I close my eyes, he goes up in flames again, blazing in the black of my mind. He burns bright, endlessly, his silent wail starved of oxygen.

I open my eyes and the black hole is hovering above me. It widens, dilating like a pupil.

Here are the facts: I am thirty-three, almost a year into a job in Silicon Valley, waiting for the truth of my life to crack open and reveal itself.

Here, I am surrounded by all of the signs of money crushing the life out of a place: the rich live inside tall town homes, the poor live in faded dirty tents if they are lucky, there are boarded-up businesses next to new juice bars, people either defecating in the streets or buying gourmet groceries, eating at overpriced restaurants or out of the dumpsters in the back alley. It's a city of extremes.

The city is full of Believers. The Believers want to be here, were born to be here. They come from the Ivy League and throw their entire beings into technology. Their eyes glow as if pixelated. Their pulses thrum from stocks, driverless cars, phones that collect the data of their lives in digital dashboards reporting: songs listened to, steps taken, places visited, workouts completed, hours slept.

Those of us who aren't Believers are here in an attempt to heave ourselves up out of dying towns, out of in-state colleges, out of lower-class pasts and into the upper strata of wealth. We've come here to reinvent ourselves, with our families pushing us forward, their hands on our backs, urging us to go west, to strike gold.

But out here, out west, there are endless hours of commuting, constant emails and notifications, top secret projects, impossible deadlines. Whether you're a Believer or not, the very pressure of the atmosphere in San Francisco changes you, molds you, shapes you into a new breed of worker. It has changed me.

To survive here, I have split myself in two: my true self and my false self. My fake self rises up to take over when the demands are too great. Maybe there must always be two of us—our real selves and the ones we create to survive in the world as it is.

In my first days here, I thought I was enough. But life moved too quickly for me to stay ahead: I struggled with deadlines, over-slept, performed poorly. Then, after a work event, a girl from our sales team pressed the first bag of white powder into my palm.

"It's how we all keep up," she said, her pupils black saucers. "You clearly need it."

The drugs make me sharper, clearer, more in control. I snort one line each morning, a ritual, a new version of the first cup of coffee. Now, I complete presentations in record time. I work for fifteen hours without stopping for food, and I excel. Even better, the drugs shrink the black hole. It winnows to a speck when the cocaine takes over. When I'm not working, I get lost in screens, like everyone else here: laptop, phone, tablet, television.

The alternative is too terrifying. Sober, with the screens tucked away, a great ache surfaces. In the awful stillness, I can hear the deafening river of melancholy roaring through the dark red cave of my heart.

black hole

/'blak 'hōl/

noun

1. a region of space having a gravitational field so intense that no matter or radiation can escape.
2. a place where people or objects disappear without a trace.

e.g., Portals to danger, nothingness, mystery, evil, other dimensions, the unknown, the mystical void, death, the end of the world as we know it.

Physicists came to call them black holes because they were impossible to explain. There is no adequate literal phrase for black holes—they exist outside the realm of human understanding. Language fails us, so we personify the phenomena. Black holes: eat, ingest, suck, spew, devour, expand, grow. We make them familiar in order to understand them, to reduce our fear of what is beyond this life.

There is safety in metaphors. The truth is far more terrifying: Black holes are confrontations with the collapse of space and time. They are a reckoning with both the infinite and death, two forces that always hover above me, never letting me out of their sight.

But I keep trying to understand, to go beyond the metaphor.

I read the articles, I keep up with the research, I wait for the day a discovery will make sense of the black hole living alongside me.

e.g., The black hole has been with me for as long as I can remember, a dark dot on the film of my life.

When I came out of my mother, the black hole must have followed, tethered to her, just like me. The doctor must have unknowingly cut two cords that day: one red, one black.

The black hole is at its most powerful when I'm alone. When I'm around other people, it tends to stay small, shrinks down to a small point. But if the melancholy gets too great, if it rises up and overtakes me, the black hole swells, a rotating mass that blocks out the world. It smells sweet and metallic, like what astronauts report when they describe the smell of outer space: notes of welded silver, raspberries, burned meat.

When the black hole expands, it eclipses my heart and mind, sucks all joy and light from my body. The black hole sings and holds a single note, the song of my name. It might seem like it would be easy to resist it. But it's impossible not to hear the call into its depths. It is the siren song of the void.

The black hole is quiet in the early morning. It is as tired as I am. Before the sun comes up, the workday ritual: scalding shower, soaping skin, drying hair, applying makeup, brushing teeth, snorting a line, grabbing my bag, locking the door, and dragging my body down the stairs to the street. Then the drugs wake up my blood.

Outside, the fog is heavy, dark, thick. I still haven't gotten used to it. The mist makes the streets look eerie, haunted, unreal.

A few feet away, the man who lives beneath my window is snoring, wrapped in a hunter green blanket, his bare feet resting on the cold sidewalk. My stomach twists at the sight of his skin against concrete. The street is full of people under unzipped sleeping bags or tattered comforters.

This morning I do nothing for the man who sleeps beneath my window or any of the others. The sheer number of people who need help paralyzes me. Most of the time I look away.

I pull out my phone and press a few buttons. Two minutes later, a black car with tinted windows pulls up. I slide into the back seat, and the driver navigates the steep hills of the city. The black hole hangs above the seat beside me.

"Where you heading today?" the driver asks.

I know he can see where I'm going in the app, but he's trying to make conversation. I try to be polite.

"To the Valley."

"You work there?"

"Unfortunately."

"Lots of you here now."

"Lots of who?"

"Tech people. Valley people. Changing the city."

"I think everywhere is changing now."

"It was better before. I've been here for twelve years."

"I suppose everywhere was better twelve years ago."

"It's different, believe me. Changed more. It's worse here, rotten."

"Oh."

It is too early for this. I fall silent so he knows it. He turns up the bright song playing on the radio, ending the conversation. I absorb the chorus: a flood of boss bitch affirmations repeated by a woman over a hollow, hypnotic beat.

For a moment, the song lifts me. The melody and the drugs make me feel like a Believer: *I can do it. I can do anything today. I am great at my job. I am a great worker. I am one of the best.*

It almost works, but it stops just short. The feeling never lasts. The black hole spins once, a giant eye rolling at me.

On the train platform, the men and women stand with their faces melting into their phones. Everyone is so similar that my vision blurs, as if I am surrounded by the same man and woman, multiplied and reflected to infinity by a circle of mirrors.

The 6 a.m. express train pulls into the station. This train skips stops to get us to work faster. We file into the silver mouth, then find seats in the metal belly. The black hole is the size of a fist, occupying the space between me and a young woman in the next seat. She is a Believer. She stares straight ahead, sitting so motionless that I catch myself waiting for her next breath.

My phone vibrates with a new message. It is from the chef I have been dating for a few months.

Thinking about you and the other night. XO.

A charge electrifies my limbs, surpassing the cocaine high. The right man desiring you is a hard drug. *Can't wait to see you again*, I type, then hit send.

For a split second, I feel human again remembering his hands on me, the way we moved our bodies as one, my head on his chest after. A sweet ache grows, that rare and brief feeling at the borderline of joy.

But the train jolts forward, shattering the sensation. We snake past: junkyards full of busted metal, worn-down bamboo gardens, abandoned car lots, the grinning strip mall teeth of the suburbs, the doors of coffee shops and gas stations opening for the day, capitalism in slow morning bloom.

On the train, the commuters: open emails, play games, text lovers, swipe right. I try to resist the pull of my own phone, but it is impossible. I check my emails, answer a work question, then click on the headlines.

New Virus Spreading through Europe

Ousted Epidemiologist Says His Warnings Were Ignored

Homelessness and Housing: Can the City Find a Solution?

Half Sisters Found Dead under Local Bridge

I click the first headline. The short article details a strange illness that spreads rapidly. The thought of it scares me until a cramp pinches my lower abdomen. I check the date: my period is a few days late.

At conception, cells multiply to create a child. Cells could be multiplying inside of me right now, a red mass dividing itself over and over again until it can: breathe, hear, see, walk, talk, read, write, consume, work.

The train picks up speed. The faster we go, the more the landscape blurs. The more the landscape blurs, the more I do. We go faster and faster, until I am only a blur with the word *mother* pulsing beneath my skin.

mother

/ˈməTHər/

noun
1. a woman in relation to her child or children.

verb
1. bring up (a child) with care and affection.

e.g., In the beginning, I almost didn't know my mother's face. The black hole would hover between us, eclipsing her. In a way, then, it was the black hole that raised me, using my mother's body as a proxy.

Our thin townhouse was beige with dark blue shutters. Two gigantic gray power plant stacks rose up behind the woods near my house, endlessly churning perfect white clouds into the sky. The small creek nestled in the trees behind our house often ran fluorescent yellow. No one knew why. Our parents had nuclear theories.

Before my brother was born, it was only my mother, my father, and me.

My father was stoic, a cheap marble statue. He often seemed to be in another world, reading either the newspaper or a book, with me but not with me. We were alone together. At certain moments, he would turn soft and kind.

But my mother? A wasp, the queen, bigger than the rest of us, the only one with a stinger.

———

e.g., Saturday morning, I was pinned to my bed by the black hole swirling above me. I was too young to understand it then, and it often terrified me. Then my mother's hand was in my hair, yanking me from the bed.

"Time to clean," she said.

My mother's anger had a distinct buzzing noise.

The vacuum was too tall for me, but I wrapped my hands around its thin, metal neck.

"Make nice shapes on the carpet."

I moved the big vacuum in small patterns over the beige carpet in the living room. I did it just how she taught me. The black hole watched over me from above.

Outside, the other children emerged from their homes to play in the sprinklers that shot sparkling arcs of water into the air. It was, I realized, summer.

"Keep cleaning," my mother said.

e.g., My mother stung and stung. Her words stung. Her fury stung. Her palm stung across my skin. Some part of love must be the stinging.

After enough of the red welts, you start to change. Eventually, you begin to hide. You stay in your room, quiet. Eventually, after enough stings, you learn to avoid the wasp altogether. Eventually, you grow up and move as far away as you can. You might even put an entire country between yourself and the wasp queen.

We detach our faces from our phones and rise up when the train reaches a certain station. We spill out onto the sidewalk of a wealthy town overrun with the headquarters of every major tech company. The streets are lined with palm trees and boutiques, but even here, blanketed bodies dot the doorways.

I fall into the throng of Believers. We cross the train tracks and board a white shuttle with black tinted windows and our company logo on the side: stars and bits of code that spell out VOYAGER.

On the shuttle, the logo is everywhere: T-shirts, sweatshirts, hats, book bags, key chains, water bottles, phone cases, puffy vests. I don't wear the logo at all. My outfit: a denim jacket over a cheap black dress and black clogs. My legs, four days unshaven, dotted with random dark bruises I don't remember getting, peek out from beneath the hem. Here, these are acts of rebellion.

The shuttle pulls out of the lot and rumbles over the asphalt, jostling our bodies. I hate this part: sitting on the cramped bus as adults, too large for the seats, the way I can't stop my knees from brushing up against the knees of the Believer next to me.

We drive through downtown and onto a larger service road. A weak river flows alongside the thoroughfare. Next to the river is a circle of tents. The men who live in them wash their clothes in the water or sit on a makeshift bridge built of plywood. If you squint, you might mistake them for men gone fishing.

The same feeling I had in the city returns, stronger now. Seeing their lives along the river makes my stomach twinge.

We pass strings of RVs and campers on both sides of the road. The RVs are white or beige, striped in oranges, reds, browns, many faded from the sun, windows shaded by sheets hung for privacy.

My stomach lurches again, from empathy or guilt or pregnancy or all three.

It's impossible not to imagine the people living inside the RVs. An engineer at VOYAGER named Jeremy lives in a blue RV parked in our company lot. Everyone talks about Jeremy in hushed voices, a tone of reverence for this pale blond man with dark eyes, his body toned from drinking unfamiliar supplements. Everyone says Jeremy is frugal and smart. Everyone says he is dedicated to the company.

I have a daydream: I sneak into his RV while he is in the office and examine his possessions, smell his pillows and sheets, open his drawers and cabinets, ravenous with one question: *How does a person live when their life has been shrunken down to almost nothing?*

I check my bank balance on my phone. The figure has grown. But after taxes, it isn't nearly as much as I thought it would be. It's still enough to make my body relax until the rent check wipes out my account. Here's the sick truth: the money makes me feel safe, the bad parts of the world kept at bay, a protection, at least for now.

The shuttle turns down a small service road. The weak river grows into the bay, which glints beneath the sun on the water:

choppy, tide high. The path along the bay is lined with purple flowers in bloom. If I focus on the water and the flowers, everything is beautiful. I only have to cut my vision off at the edges.

"Next stop: VOYAGER," the driver says. VOYAGER is a unicorn start-up valued at $16 billion for its opaque use of data to target users, driving them to make purchases online. I am the head writer on the marketing team.

The shuttle pulls into the lot. We file out, our shoulders touching again. The tide of my melancholy surges.

Outside, the pristine glass buildings reflect the sky back at itself. Handsome men in plain clothes climb out of luxury electric sports cars. Women in athleisure power walk beneath the green palm fronds. Caterers unload boxes of cellophane-wrapped sandwiches and bright fruits, shining in the morning sun like jewels. Everything shimmers: the grass, the flowers, the miniature man-made waterfall on a patio furnished with lounge chairs and hammocks. Another shuttle arrives, opening its doors and spilling more of us out onto the campus.

The black hole is at the edge of my vision, levitating over the vibrant green grass. With each step toward the building, my dread grows—and the black hole does, too, blocking out the sun, forcing itself into the scenes of my life.

A brighter song begins on my earbuds, one with poppy energy, with the sparkle of the new mirrored buildings and blue skies and the bay, the beautiful bay. I let the music drown everything out. I pretend none of this is happening to me. I pretend this is someone else's life.

work

/ˈwərk/

noun

1. activity involving mental or physical effort done in order to achieve a purpose or result.
2. a task or tasks to be undertaken; something a person or thing has to do.

verb

1. be engaged in physical or mental activity in order to achieve a purpose or result, especially in one's job; do work.

e.g., "The job doesn't stop," my father said once on a family vacation when he was between work calls.

"I can handle it," my mother said after vomiting in the trash can next to her bed, her watering eyes hollowed out from fever. "I'm going into the office."

"Sometimes, you have to give the beast what it needs," my father said before he left my tenth birthday party to handle an emergency at the office.

I didn't know what an emergency at the office meant. I imagined papers and pens in violent revolt, important deals bursting into flames, the company as a needy child demanding time and attention. There always seemed to be something invisible happening:

sales closed or lost, power moves or big losses, negotiations or random lawsuits.

The language my parents used at the dinner table was foreign, from a distant shore, another country.

"We're about to close on the quarter and we've got to move the needle," my father said, his mouth full of cheap steak.

"We need a win-win before they move the goalposts," my mother said. "I'm getting fucked from every fucking angle here, even with the low-hanging fruit."

"Fuck these fucking fuckers," my father said. "You don't need to boil the ocean here. It's not your fault they're churning."

I imagined: a football field, an orchard, the blue sea, a tub of butter.

In the end, it was endless meetings, corporate pressure, profit goals. It was nowhere near as exotic as it seemed at the dinner table. When you're young, every part of life seems big and monumental. Once older, you can see it for what it is: smaller pieces of a larger game you have no choice but to play.

I am my mother in the mirror beneath the yellow light of the office bathroom: dark half-moons beneath my eyes, pores large as buckets, lips a thin, grim line. I work with what I have. I fluff my limp, drugstore auburn hair, wipe away the smudged black mascara from beneath my flat brown eyes, pinch my cheeks, bite my lips until they redden to bring the life back into my face. If I just keep making adjustments, eventually I could be beautiful.

"Morning!" someone says.

She appears in the mirror next to me: younger, blond hair, bright blue eyes, glowing tan, the next generation of tech, the embodiment of the Valley, radiating probiotics and spirulina. Her name is Cat or Julie or Jennifer or Lindsay. I can never keep the new girls from Sales straight.

My fake self slides over me like a mask.

"Good morning!" I say like a Believer.

"Love your dress!" she chirps back.

I give her outfit a quick once-over: a gray woven T-shirt with the company logo, raw denim jeans, and mint-green sneakers, which are sustainable or tied to a charity. They are likely saving a tree in the rain forest right now because of her shoes.

"Oh my god, it's from forever ago! Thank you, though!" I say on cue. "I love your shoes!"

"Thank you! Oh my god, I know you won't believe this, but

they're made from recycled soda cans. So, it's, like, yes, they are stylish. But also? We're doing something *good*."

"Totally! You have to do something *good*."

Her existence underscores all of my flaws: my flabby stomach, wide nose, all of me revealed as uneven in the face of her flat stomach, full lips, bright eyes, perfect symmetry.

"How's your day going?" she asks.

I pause. It's not even 8 a.m. and my day has only just begun. This is a trick question. She is coming at me from every angle. I am under siege, in a war, the enemy attacking at dawn.

"Honestly, *great*! So many meetings, you know? Big day!" my fake self says, eyeing her reflection. I worry my breath stinks. Can she smell it?

"Same here! Such a big day. Getting in early to get out ahead of it, girl!"

"Girl, same! It's so worth it! We're so lucky!"

"I know! Totally worth it. We're the luckiest! See you out there," she says as she vanishes from the frame.

My shoulders go limp from the exertion of my performance. The mirror and the double sinks and the stalls and the table of toiletries warp as if I am inside of a looking glass. Ten hours of work stretch out ahead of me. I feel the pressure against my skin. I must not make a single mistake.

In the mirror, the black hole spins behind my head, expanding from a small dot to a dark halo. A new question echoes in my mind: *Am I a husk now, too?*

The open office floor plan is a form of strangulation. White desks stand in perfect rows on blue-gray carpet. The lighting has been scientifically proven to increase our productivity by 14 percent. Giant concrete-colored couches dot the room, an invitation to sit and relax. But I have never seen anyone sit on the sofas. The subtext is clear: we must never relax.

The layout means everyone can see us as we walk, eat, think, breathe, work. Every move is on display. The office is two hands around my throat and an invisible eye, spying, monitoring, measuring our productivity.

There is only one positive: once I'm inside the office, the black hole stays small and quiet, as if even it knows I have to focus.

I make my way to my desk in measured steps, sucking in my stomach, attempting to be poised, careful not to make a sound.

A dream from a few nights ago suddenly returns to me: my heart was pulled from my throat, my body heaving until it emerged through my stretched lips. Then my heart was suspended in the air before me: wet and pulsing, attached to red veins that ran like umbilical cords from my mouth.

My throat tightens at the memory, like I'm being choked with my real heart. I swallow the sensation.

I open my laptop and my fake self springs into action: sending emails, answering messages, organizing files, reviewing the progress of my projects. I stare at my screen with both intensity and intention. Someone, somewhere, is measuring each of my keystrokes, which websites I visit, the exact number of hours I'm active each day.

I know what the great invisible eye likes to see, and I deliver. My father taught me everything I know about work:

"Say three smart things in every meeting, then shut the fuck up."

"They always have more money than they're telling you they have."

"Keep a list of the three people whose graves you would piss on if given the chance."

"Always watch the CEO. And listen. Always."

So I watch the watchers. I listen to the listeners. I monitor the CEO closely. This CEO speaks in the blue glow of code.

```
01000101 01111000 01100011 01100101 01101100
01101100 01100101 01101110 01100011 01100101
00101100 00100000 01110010 01100001 01110000
01101001 01100100 00101101 01100110 01101001
01110010 01100101 00100000 01110000 01110010
01101111 01100100 01110101 01100011 01110100
01101001 01110110 01101001 01110100 01111001
00101100 00100000 01101100 01100101 01100001
01101110 00100000 01100010 01101111 01100100
01101001 01100101 01110011 00101100 00100000
01101111 01110000 01110100 01101001 01101101
01101001 01111010 01100001 01110100 01101001
01101111 01101110 00101100 00100000 01101100
01101111 01100111 01101001 01100011 00101100
00100000 01110000 01100101 01100001 01101011
00100000 01110000 01100101 01110010 01100110
01101111 01110010 01101101 01100001 01101110
01100011 01100101 00101110 00100000
```

Excellence, rapid-fire productivity, lean bodies, optimiza-
tion, logic, peak performance. Don't stop. Never stop. Keep
working. You are better than everyone else. You don't need
food. You don't need sugar. Work harder. Work harder. Work
harder. Grow beyond what you are. Transcend your fears.
Leave your heart at home. All that matters is your output.

His words are built into the air, invisible spores, our company culture a one-man contagion.

I almost lose myself in the thrum of productivity. But beneath checking items off of my to-do list, beneath the mask of my fake self, a sound bangs inside of my chest like a drum: my heart chanting *no, no, no.*

ergosphere

/ˈərɡōˌsfir/

noun

1. a postulated region around a black hole, from
   which energy could still escape.
2. a region located outside a rotating black hole's
   outer event horizon.

e.g., The ergosphere is the outer region of a black hole. It is a cosmic whirlpool—any object within the ergosphere is forced to move in the same direction in which the black hole is spinning, even space-time. But once sucked into the whirlpool, it is possible, with enough velocity, for an object to escape the ergosphere. From here, you could theoretically escape from a black hole alive.

e.g., I had figured out the black hole's core behaviors: despite its threatening presence, it never sucked anything up, it never touched me, it only came close enough to scare me or block my vision. When it drew close to me, I could feel the dark warmth it radiated.

I made a list of facts:

- The outer area of a black hole is exceedingly
  hot, but its center is freezing cold.

- There are four types of black holes: stellar, intermediate, supermassive, and miniature.

- Black holes have three properties: mass, charge, and spin.

- Miniature black holes may have formed immediately after the big bang. Rapidly expanding space could have squeezed some regions into tiny, dense black holes smaller than our sun.

I wondered if the black hole trailing me had been around that long, since the beginning of our known world.

e.g., My research began in high school. I devoured books and scientific journals, trying to make sense of what was happening. All the while, the black hole whirled above me while I sat alone in my bedroom.

"What are you up to?" my father asked, popping his head through my open bedroom door. The black hole shrank when he appeared.

"Researching," I said.

"Black holes again? What's gotten into you?"

"They're fascinating, you know? Listen to this," I said, reading from the book: "'A black hole is created by the death of a massive star that collapses inward upon itself, and the star's outer layers are blown away.'"

"Okay, you got me. That's pretty cool," my father said. "But what's inside?"

"Well . . . space-time becomes so warped that it twists in on itself, ripping a hole through the very fabric of reality," I said, my head beginning to ache. "Space and time switch places. The book says the laws of physics as we know them no longer apply."

"So what happens if you enter one?"

"They're still trying to figure that out."

My father shook his head. "Listen, I'm just here to tell you to come down to dinner. Good luck with the rest of all this shit."

He stepped out of frame, and it was just me and the black hole, which spiraled wider. I stared into the abyss and wondered, not for the first or the last time, what would become of me if I let myself fall inside.

e.g., The obsession followed me into adulthood. Almost every day, a new finding emerged about black holes: how they looked, how they behaved, their implications for the universe. I could hardly keep up.

The headlines I memorized:

Astronomers Capture the Most Detailed Photo
of a Black Hole Ever

Black Holes May Have Existed Since the Beginning of Time

Black Holes and Dark Matter May Be the Same

The first headline appeared on my phone while I was on the train to the office in my first weeks in California. I clicked the link excitedly, pulse racing from drugs and hope: maybe the black hole would look similar to mine, maybe the image would give some clue about the void that followed me each day, maybe I could finally solve the black puzzle that haunted me.

But it was nothing so meaningful. Black holes don't emit or

reflect light, so the photograph only captured the gas swirling around the black hole. The picture showed a hot red blur with a dark spot in the center fifty-five million light years away.

It didn't look much like my black hole, which was the darkest black I had ever seen, its depths still maddeningly unfathomable.

e.g., The rest of the research fascinated me, even if it didn't entirely explain my situation.

One of the documentaries featured astronomers and astrophysicists in sensible black turtlenecks and understated sweaters. They stood before blackboards covered in calculations that made my head spin. They quoted Stephen Hawking and Carl Sagan amid footage of swirling galaxies and black holes colliding.

Then astrophysicist Janna Levin was on the screen: "Supermassive black holes in the centers of galaxies are structuring, shaping, sculpting the way galaxies form. They're also telling us something about our future because that's where we're likely to end up: in the center of black holes."

I turned off the documentary and stared into the depths of the abyss in my living room.

In the office, I type what I am meant to type. I develop new ideas, run reports, collect data, create decks with slides that tell narratives, because everyone wants narratives, they are expecting a story, a dynamic story with empathy and energy.

Today I write a report on how to capture and keep people's attention online: how to leverage techniques first used on gamblers and how to appeal to our human love of games to encourage a user to click the buy button for increased gratification and keep them coming back again and again and again. I write about the colors of buttons, the optimal utilization of text, where the eye tends to land on a screen, how to subtly scam the human into being tracked, into the sales funnel, as if through a chute, like a cow on the way to slaughter, to the right place, to the right action, at the right time.

My mind deteriorates in the blue glow. Time itself becomes elastic. My brain goes blank.

My boss, Sasha, comes in an hour late. She sits with her back to me, a back that I've memorized: thin from disordered eating and anxiety, muscular from yoga and Pilates, a telltale hump from years of hunching over a laptop.

"Morning, Sasha," I say.

She nods, not turning from her screen.

Sasha has dark eyes and dark brown hair that she occasionally shocks with bright blonde or caramel highlights. She wears yoga pants and thin bracelets around her bony wrists that advertise her spirituality in gold script: *Buddhism*, *Zen*, *Bad Bitch*. She drives a hideous bright green car. She either ignores me or berates me.

She is a cofounder of the company, with men making up the rest of the C-level. She has an origin story that plays well in the media, so she repeats it regularly:

"I was born in Russia, very poor, raised without running water or electricity. Then I came to America for college, and here is where I cofounded VOYAGER. That is the American dream."

I don't know if her story is real. I can't figure her out. A coldness emanates from her center. She reminds me of the black hole in that way. There must be suffering inside of her, a wild, unruly pain. But it is buried beneath layers of false confidence and the jargon she repeats from online leadership courses and the CEO:

"Women should not touch their hair in meetings."

"Have you tried a juice cleanse?"

"When you're presenting to an audience, try wearing a leather jacket to give off an air of confidence."

"Eating too much sugar leads to poor presentations."

family

/ˈfam(ə)lē/

noun
1. a group of one or more parents and their children living together as a unit.
2. all the descendants of a common ancestor.

e.g., A family is a set of people tied to each other by blood and history. Certain histories require us to examine their purpose. Certain families require us to understand a crooked lineage. The word *family* might send a shudder of dismay through a certain person.

e.g., Then my mother was pregnant. She grew full with my brother, her ankles swelling. She was too tired, then, to sting. Instead, she ravenously ate common fruits: strawberries, raspberries, peaches, plums.

Her belly grew and grew. Sometimes my father put his hands on her stomach. His eyes were full of wonder and dread in equal measure. Sometimes the black hole hovered in front of my mother's stomach and she seemed to be carrying the abyss.

In retrospect, my mother and the black hole made the same sound, that low, relentless buzz. Maybe I have always had two black holes trailing me.

———

e.g., One day my mother began screaming. Suddenly the house was full of commotion. Then we were in the beige station wagon, then the hospital with its pale blues and greens, a strange nod to the sea.

I sat on a blue plastic chair. Once in a while my father emerged from the room that held my mother, to bring me snacks from a vending machine. I didn't know what was happening inside of the room. My mother kept screaming. The black hole hung beside me over its own blue plastic chair. Birth was a mystery, but by then I was familiar with pain.

After that, they let me into my mother's hospital room. After that, I had a brother. He was small and pink as a pig. He had big brown eyes and thick brown hair. He peered up at me and wrapped his small hand around my fingers, a strange new creature that I immediately loved without knowing how or why.

e.g., The years between my brother and me built a distance into our relationship. I was never quite sure what to do with him. We had sprouted from the same base but grew in separate directions. My mother stung him less; I always noticed that. She let him sleep in on Saturdays, never raised her voice, her hand was never in his hair. As I watched her love him, the sadness inside of me grew larger.

e.g., There were normal moments: a first Holy Communion, a Girl Scout troop, a babysitter, school, summer vacations, a group of girls who were my friends, books, art class.

But I was only half present, half alive, even then, even that young.

"Stop staring into the distance," my mother frequently snapped. "You never have your wits about you."

It was true. I was distracted. The black hole was always sliding into the scene, eclipsing entire moments, blotting out giant swaths of the world, spinning, buzzing, its familiar metallic scent forcing me to wonder if there might be something more beyond this life.

e.g., I never asked my mother if a black hole trailed her, too. I came close once, on a cool spring day. We were in the cramped shared backyard of our townhouse. In the distance, over the treetops, the power plant churned its perfect clouds into the sky. Inside, men split atoms to make energy. My friends' fathers worked inside the belly of the plant. I pictured the energy they made as orange lightning erupting from blue orbs.

In my high school that week, we'd had drills for what to do if the plant melted down: our bodies would curl up beneath desks or we would be shuttled to neighboring towns. We hoped the buses would move faster than the leaking energy. The meltdowns would either look bright as fireworks, or else dark, as if the mouth of the black hole had consumed not just me but everything.

e.g., My mother was drinking wine in the early afternoon that day. I knew not to mention the hour. Her profile against the bright blue sky: short drugstore-brown hair, pert nose, cheeks hollowed with age, bags beneath her eyes, laying out my future. She was short, which added to the tension between us. I inherited my height from my father. I inherited my mother's strange toes and large hands. I cannot get them off of me. Some things are permanent.

The black hole had grown more demanding. Whenever I was alone, it would rise up like an awful sun, spinning, calling me into its center. I couldn't tell if it wanted to destroy me or if it was offering another future, a different path, a new dimension.

"I get sad sometimes," I said to my mother, our bare feet in the patchy, half-dead grass, the sun burning away above our heads. "I get so sad sometimes that it's physically painful. Sometimes I hope the earth cracks open or the sea sweeps me away."

"Sad?" she asked. "Well, I don't want you to be sad, of course, you know I don't. But the earth? The sea? What's the use in all of that? What sea? We're nowhere near the ocean."

"Doesn't it overwhelm you sometimes? To be alive? Don't you sometimes feel like at any moment you could be torn away from yourself? From your life?"

"I don't know what you're getting at. You're too attached to your own feelings. Life isn't so complicated as you make it for yourself."

The words were her stinger, aiming for the heart.

My mother sipped from her glass, the pink wine refracting the light. I wanted to say the words *black hole* but I couldn't force them from my mouth. I wasn't sure I would get an answer anyway. If she did have a black hole trailing her, she would hide it from me. That was the nature of our relationship: a mutual hiding.

"I guess it's just different for me," I said.

"Stop all this sad sea talk. For Christ's sake. There are children dying in other countries. Go to Afghanistan and see how people live there before you walk around with all of this bullshit about the ocean taking you away."

"Afghanistan?"

"Afghanistan. They know what sadness really is. No cell phones there. Only poverty, illness, suffering. Educate yourself."

"I'm not going to Afghanistan."

"Whether you go or not, you need to get a fucking grip. And tougher skin."

I imagined myself like that: a woman with tough skin, my body covered in leather, walking through the world impenetrable, untouched by sadness or sea.

More coworkers shuffle in from the late-morning train, all of them blurring into the same person. They smile or nod, slide their earbuds in, and open up their computers. They exude enthusiasm, typing with intention—almost with pleasure. I watch their eyes come alive with purpose, their bodies poised like Olympic athletes at a starting line, all focus and determination.

I don't know what to make of these strangers I spend hours with each day. I know their smells, their eating habits, the number of times they go to the bathroom in a day, all of the information shared between friends and lovers, but we are neither.

I send what is supposedly an important email, then look over at Sasha and the rest of the team. My nerves almost get the better of me as I say, "Just heading to the bathroom."

I feel safe in the beige stall. I pull out my phone and click through social media, which the company has blocked on our laptops. I fall into the stream of updates and photographs: wrinkled babies, exotic vacations, new jobs, completed marathons, perfectly edited selfies.

I take a selfie against the wall in the bathroom, then quickly edit out the bags under my eyes and toss on a filter so I look five years younger. My phone lights up with alerts: five likes, two comments. In the rush of it, for a moment, I almost feel like I am the girl in the phone. I feel like I am the illusion.

There is, of course, no way to photograph loneliness, or any state of lack. Gray is thought to be the color of loneliness, the same color as the brain or the heart drained of blood. There is, of course, no way to photograph the black hole, which is always waiting, watching, shrinking or growing, that cruel dark mirror.

Sasha's neon-orange shoes appear in the gap between the stall door and the floor, a new line of flats made from upcycled parking cones.

"Cassie?" she says in a soft tone, her accent making my name sound more beautiful than it is.

My shoulders tense. I can't have a single moment of peace in this office, no place is safe.

"Yes? What is it?"

"Oh, nothing! When you're done, I have something for you."

"Okay, great, be right out."

I flush the unused toilet for effect and step out of the stall. Sasha looks shy and mean at the same time. She holds a white package in her outstretched hands.

"I know you have been working hard lately," she says. "And I know I don't always know how to express myself. So, I got you this."

She places the pristine box in my hands.

"Oh, thank you," I say. "That's so thoughtful. And you've been wonderful to me, truly. A mentor."

We both plaster strained smiles on our faces. I unwrap the package, sliding the tissue paper aside to reveal a white plate with gold letters spelling out *She Believed She Could and So She Did.*

I take a moment to indulge a fantasy: smashing the plate against the wall, white shards flying, bits of porcelain in our faces and hair, the small bloody gashes across our skin marking us as true sisters.

Then my fake self takes over.

"Oh god, this is beautiful!" I say. "I was just looking for a new plate for cheese and crackers."

"Exactly!" she says, her eyes wide. "Cheese and crackers! With wine!"

I visualize the gratitude of another woman, a vegan woman who does hot yoga and embraces technology and start-ups and wears the logo with pride.

"Thank you, really. It means so much to me. I'm touched."

She smiles, half a smile, almost like a real person. I picture her outside of work: on a beach, her hair glowing in the sun, not an awful person, just a repressed woman who is as miserable as I am.

"Okay, see you out there," she says as she opens the restroom door. Then she pauses and looks back at me. "By the way, your writing on the last report on digital conversion totally sucked. Redo the entire thing. I pulled it from the editorial calendar until you can fix it. We expect the best at VOYAGER, not piles of shit."

The door swings shut behind her. A wave of nausea hits me. I'd spent weeks on the project. The work was good, I know it was. But for an instant, my reality wavers: maybe I am terrible, maybe I don't deserve to be here, maybe I am a nothing.

Above us, the very galaxies rotate and collide. Stars are born and die. The whole of the universe breathes and expands. Suddenly I can see the disparity so clearly—the men bathing in the river, and me in the bathroom, holding a porcelain plate, always failing.

The office kitchen is small, causing us to bump elbows in yet another forced intimacy. The kitchen reflects the CEO's commitment to health: grain-free sprouted bread, avocados, lemons, organic low-sugar peanut butter.

The CEO rarely eats in front of us, which adds to the perception he is beyond human, a paragon of competence and control. I mirror that behavior, speaking to him in his own code. I try not to eat here if I can help it. I survive on espresso, green tea, seltzer, water with lemon, turbo cold brew specifically designed with an almost lethal amount of caffeine to jolt us all into prolonged productivity.

Someone bumps my hip. I look up and lock eyes with Jeremy. He wears a pale blue woven T-shirt, his muscles straining against the expensive absorbent fabric. I look down to avoid prolonged eye contact and notice that he has nice hands with long, slender fingers, and that is almost more intimate.

"Morning," he says. His voice is deep enough to send a small current of want down my spine.

"Morning," I say.

"You're drinking your usual, I see."

"My usual?"

"You like one Splenda in your coffee. And a splash of almond milk."

His observation makes me feel naked. Heat rushes to my cheeks.

"Yes, that's how I take it. What about you? You're always in here making concoctions with some weird powder."

"Oh, that's a rare husk from Madagascar meant to improve blood flow."

"Ah, okay, blood flow. Right. You . . . you live in that RV in the parking lot, right?"

"Yeah, that's my place."

"Cool. That's cool. Do you like living there?"

"It's all I need for now."

We fall silent.

Men like this confuse me. Do I want to have sex with him? I don't think so. But here he is, and here I am, and here is this exchange. I'm like this whenever I'm near a man: I never know what I want.

I sprinkle Splenda into my cold brew. As I leave the kitchen, I can feel his eyes on my back. It would be a lie to say I didn't want them there.

The picture windows of the office offer a panoramic view of the bay. The scenic swell of the water at high tide is receding, revealing the grimy, brown muck of the shore.

Once, walking the path along the bay, I saw a family of duck-lings paddling after their mother. I stopped and watched as they neared the water's edge. For a moment, I felt chosen by a greater force, as if a hand of light had reached through the clouds to reveal this miracle of life specifically to me. I couldn't take my eyes off those baby ducks, their small hearts beating new and wild in the world.

Out of nowhere a crow descended and snatched one of the babies. It didn't look real, but it was: the duckling in that black beak, in the air, then slammed against a rock until it went limp, the ruthlessness of nature horrifying me.

The office churns on around me. The receding water reveals: the bones of fish, rotting wood, empty chip bags, bright crushed soda cans. It feels good to see ugliness on the otherwise immaculate campus, where everything is polished to a sheen. The truth of the world bares itself when the tide goes down: devoured, used, rotting.

memory

/ˈmem(ə)rē/

noun
1. the faculty by which the mind stores and remembers information.
2. something remembered from the past; a recollection.

e.g., Maybe you cannot trust a memory. Our brains mirror technology: certain moments are overridden by bigger, more important memories. Encoding, storage, retrieval. There is only so much room in the mind.

If you asked me how I got to California, I could dig through the mental files, tunnel through time to the memories I've buried under new data. It is hard to tell which memories are correct and which have been corrupted.

e.g., The memories: a lonely plane ride across the country, a high-end hotel room, a dress and blazer for the interview, a trip to the office in the sunny back seat of the car service, all the palm trees and roses—everything always in bloom here—then sitting beneath fluorescent lights in a small conference room.

A rapid-fire succession of faces: young male deities testing my knowledge, the female HR rep asking about my biggest accomplishments and failures, my potential boss, Sasha, calling in via video from Bali.

For the duration of the interview, the black hole floated just to the right, a freckle in the periphery of the scene.

e.g., It was during the whiteboard challenge that I became a demon. The panel of interviewers included a few of the small gods and Sasha's face, humongous on a flat screen.

"We want to see how your mind works," one of them said. "Here's the challenge: create a plan for launching an entirely new product."

Then the fake version of me took over and pulled out all the stops. She grabbed a black marker and blasted the board with ideas, the felt tip on a manic journey across a slippery dry-erase road. She detailed it all: case studies, email blasts, in-app notifications, a drip campaign, banner ads, billboards, bus stop takeovers, a press release translated into nineteen languages and distributed in every country worth the money.

She sold herself; my god, it was a thing of beauty. The heads on the panel nodded with appreciation at her work, her energy, her brilliance.

Once the interview ended, she was gone.

e.g., Later, energy spent, I called my father from the cloud of my hotel bed.

He was stocking shelves at the grocery store, his retirement job. We pretended he worked there because he liked to organize. But the truth was my parents weren't good with money and couldn't live off his 401(k). I pictured him kneeling in the spice aisle in his maroon logo polo, khaki shorts, and white off-brand Costco sneakers, his hands full of glass bottles rattling with cinnamon sticks and peppercorns.

"How'd it go, baby girl?"

"Don't call me that."

"You give 'em the old charm?"

"I think so, I did. But you never know what secret test of theirs I might have failed."

"Well, let's hope you got it."

"Would I really take it? Would I really move here?"

"I mean . . . there's nothing here for you anymore. What else you got going on?"

In truth, nothing. I'd been at the same job for years, coasting in a comfortable position writing marketing copy at a huge software company. They promoted me every few years like clockwork. I could get lost in the thousands of other employees. I was bored, stagnating. We both knew if I didn't take this start-up job, I would never become anything other than what I already was.

"I think . . . I think I'd take it."

"In a heartbeat. You'd be a goddamn moron not to. No dummies in this family, all right? I gotta go—this rosemary has to get on the shelf. Love you."

"Love you."

In the corner of the hotel room, the black hole swelled and hummed until the sound became a lullaby, until I faded into sleep.

e.g., Sasha called me three days later from Brazil. I could hear the sea crashing against the shore in the background. I could almost smell salt and sand, brine rising in my throat.

"We are so excited to extend the position to you," Sasha said. "We'll pay for your move, and we've crafted a package with generous stock, plus a signing bonus."

My heart kicked in my chest. The red valves opened and closed faster, speeding my pulse. I imagined my near future: flying across the country to stay this time, becoming new, starting over, a blank canvas.

"Thank you so much! This news is so exciting," I said, parroting her words back to her automatically.

"It was a unanimous decision. Everyone is so excited to see what you can do for us."

She kept saying *excited*. I was excited. She was excited. Everyone was excited. It was, it seemed, very exciting.

"Can I have a day to think about it?"

The line went silent. The black hole buzzed in my other ear, eavesdropping.

"A day?" she asked, her voice razorlike now, sharp.

"Yes, just a day."

"Think it through? We're doubling your current salary. It should be an immediate yes."

"Well, I just need to think it through and make sure this is the right move for me."

"I . . . yes, yes, take a day. I'll have the offer emailed over."

"Thank you so much. Thank you, I am so excited."

It was late afternoon. I climbed into bed, the only place I felt safe. The sun beamed orange slits of light through the blinds. The black hole hung over me as I imagined myself in the new life. The prospect was so overwhelming that my body shut down and I fell into a deep sleep.

e.g., This dream I remember: a room made of pink-and-white frosted cake and lined with gigantic mirrors, fondant scalloped walls, icing-laced chandeliers glowing above me.

I reached out a finger and brought a dollop of frosting to my mouth. It dissolved on my tongue, the sugar exquisite. I turned, as if I knew the place, and stepped onto an escalator with sugar-lined railings. There was no sign of the black hole. I was calm, at peace, savoring a newfound sweetness.

At the top of the escalator, I made my way to a single window, its edges decorated with elaborate pink frosting swirls. Outside, as far as I could see, was a dark grease-slicked bog flecked with fires burning red. The heat of the fires grew closer. A terrible foreboding hung over the scene.

e.g., An hour later, I woke up in a cold sweat to my phone ringing.

"Hello?"

"Cassie, it's the CEO of VOYAGER. I spoke with Sasha about our offer."

My heart stopped. His voice sounded like money and business. He sounded like my father.

"Oh, hi. I don't think we had the chance to meet during my interview."

"We didn't. But Sasha told me you were dragging your feet on the position."

My arms went numb with fear. My heart began to pound. The black hole swelled, its sweet metallic scent filled my nostrils.

"Oh, I'm not dragging my feet, it's that . . . moving across the country is a big deal for me. I'm very excited about the offer, I just wanted to sit with it for a minute."

"We were really hoping you'd accept the offer immediately.

Sasha assures me that you're the person for the job, but we have other candidates lined up."

"It's a great opportunity. I promise I'll get back to you soon."

"I'm confident you will make the right choice, and quickly. We don't waste time here at VOYAGER. Nice speaking with you. We'll see you soon."

The next morning, I accepted the job. Or maybe it was my fake self, the other me. It's hard to tell where I end and where she begins.

e.g., If the brain is elastic and memory is faulty, maybe all of these stories are wrong. Maybe it happened a different way altogether. Maybe I was happy and I just forget that now.

My mind begins to unravel during annual sexual harassment training. My coworkers and I sit at a large patio table beneath the winter sun during a break from the sessions. Throughout the morning, men in casual blazers and one woman in a modest dress stood before us in a conference room defining *boundaries* and *consent* as if they were new concepts.

Now, meaningless conversations buzz around me about softball leagues, Pilates, bridal parties, tee times, electric cars, protein powders, stock options.

A platter of ripe fruits sits in the center of the table: pomegranate, dragon fruit, passion fruit, guava, figs, star fruit, and others I can't identify.

"I am so sick of dragon fruit," a man in a VOYAGER T-shirt says. "Every single time, they send dragon fruit. What the fuck?"

My colleagues peck away at the colorful array. We didn't have exotic produce back home, and I can't take my eyes off the platter. The hues and patterns dazzle me: pink and white speckles, mottled yellow, bright orange, deep purple, prickly green. Some of the fruits require special techniques to devour: the splitting of rinds, the removal of pits, the scooping of innards.

"I'm sick of it, too," a woman in a black athletic pullover says. "They always give us the same shit."

It must take enormous effort to produce the platters: the fruits growing on lush, tropical trees and bushes a world away, picked by underpaid hands, and then transported thousands of miles, ripening on their way to our gaping mouths.

"At least the mango is edible this time," someone else says.

All of their blank faces, bland in the bright sun, blur into one again.

"I wonder if this quarter is going to be rough with that new virus going around," one of my coworkers says.

My eyes are glued to the pomegranate, to the spilt scarlet seeds and bloody juice spattered across the bone white of the plate.

"What do you think of the virus? Is it bullshit or are you worried?" another coworker asks the table.

"It's all bullshit," someone says.

"I read that a man in Paris died from it yesterday," I say. "Scary."

The black hole expands above us, blocking out the sun and casting a shadow over me, but no one else seems to notice. I am the only one sitting in the new darkness.

"That's Paris, though," someone says. "It's different there. You know? They all live on top of each other."

"I'm not worried," a coworker says definitively, as if a judge making a ruling, as if deciding for us all. "We're fine here."

The black hole rotates and contracts, as if in warning. But I'm barely paying attention. The pomegranate seeds glisten in the sun like freshly pulled teeth. The rich ruby color absorbs me. I lose myself again in the fruit, in the lush electric red of life.

———

Back in the conference room, the training session resumes.
We sit in clusters. Another generically handsome man in front
delivers the training. Men are always at the front of the room,
talking through tiny microphones clipped to their suits, making
small and then ever-larger gestures with their hands.

"As you can see, unwelcome touching in the work environment
has a detrimental impact on both parties, and the behavior puts
the company at legal risk," the man says, tenting his fingers before
spreading his arms wide. "Here's an example of what counts as
inappropriate or unwelcome touching. The buttocks, the waist,
the nape of the neck . . ."

I stare out the window. My eyes return to the abandoned
platter on the table. The uneaten fruit is a ruined still life in the
sun. The pomegranate, split open but barely eaten, shimmers a
brilliant vermillion. I feel the same color in my womb, imagining
red cells multiplying.

The black hole floats at the center of my vision, now the size
of a pomegranate.

The meeting finally ends. In my few spare minutes, I stand
outside and slowly type the word *pomegranate* into my phone.

I read the facts:

- In Greek mythology, the pomegranate was
  known as "the fruit of the dead," as it was said
  to have arisen from the blood of Adonis.

- Alongside death, the pomegranate symbolized
  fertility in ancient Greece and Rome.

- Hades, god of the underworld, infamously tricked Persephone into eating three pomegranate seeds, which obligated her to live beneath the ground with him for a few months of every year.

- According to ancient Iranian Christianity, the pomegranate was believed to be the real forbidden fruit in the Garden of Eden, not the apple.

The subject of the next meeting is top secret. The calendar invite says "New Project," with no further details. This is what the CEO does when it is time for a mission.

The big conference room is designed to impress investors: a long table made from exotic wood and tempered glass flanked by floor-to-ceiling windows offering views of the palm trees. A small refrigerator with a glass door holds rare seltzer flavors and yerba maté.

I pull out my pen and paper. In most meetings with the CEO, we are forbidden from looking at phones or laptops. We are only meant to gaze upon each other, our minds bursting with new and innovative ideas, data exchanging through the air between us.

The meeting includes me, Sasha, Jeremy, a woman from sales, and a pale Ivy Leaguer named Corbett. They call Corbett the mini-CEO. I hate him with the whole fist of my heart, his pimply skin, watery gray eyes behind thick black frames, strange accent that sounds like a synthesis of British and American tones, a voice as snotty as it is fake. A rumored chess prodigy, he was halfway through a degree in anthropology at an Ivy before the CEO poached him and he dropped out to become one of our small gods.

The CEO is at the head of the table. He is generically handsome with brown hair, dark eyes, tan skin, electric white teeth. He is like all of the Valley's CEOs: his father is a doctor or a lawyer, his mother of an unknown occupation, his wife an Ivy League doctor or full-time philanthropist.

Rumors whispered about the CEO: he drinks special smoothies instead of eating, hates bad breath, consumes no sugar, despises white bread, lifts weights in a home gym. We watch his muscles grow each day alongside his power, his prestige. We talk about him as if we are talking about royalty. We are worshipful, terrified, enthralled.

"I'm sure you're all wondering why you are here," the CEO says. "And I'm going to be very blunt. We have a situation on our hands. The very life and death of this company will depend on the success of this initiative. Let me put it simply: we must take down the competition. And as you all know, I'm talking about Nomad. Those assholes are eating our lunch."

"They're an abomination," Corbett says.

"They are. We must destroy them. And I mean *destroy,*" the CEO says. "I've invited you here because I know I can trust you. You understand how important trust is, right?"

We all nod, except the girl from sales. She is paralyzed, eyes wide.

"If you are uncomfortable with what I say next, please excuse yourself from the room. We're losing ground in key demographics. Nomad is taking our clients and smearing our name. We need to regain the upper hand—by any means necessary. Whoever remains in this room must never speak a word of these meetings or our plans to anyone outside of this group."

I pretend to look solemnly out the window at a palm tree. I don't care what we do or whom we destroy. My father says that capitalism is a chess match. We are only playing the same game of chess until we aren't, until the paychecks stop.

". . . so we'll need a war chest from a few private investors, and then we need to take action," the CEO continues. "We're calling this initiative Prometheus. And if we can do this—if we can take Nomad out—we can do anything. We will be unstoppable. We will be number one and nothing will be able to touch us. There is no doubt we will go public."

The speech almost works on me, it's that good. I imagine us destroying Nomad and going public, my stocks soaring. The thought of future wealth gives me a high in spite of myself. My fake self delivers the line my father would:

"I'm in," I say. "Let's destroy them."

The CEO's eyes light up.

"Yes!" he says. "That's the energy I want in this room. But before we go any further, does anyone need to leave? If you're going to bow out, now's the time."

The girl from sales stands up. Her face is drained of blood and papery.

"I have a lot of other work on my plate," she says, barely above a whisper. "I honestly don't think I can take on any more."

The CEO stares through her. For a moment, I wonder if he's going to hurt her. Then the tension passes, and she quietly makes her way out.

"Anyone else?" he asks. "There will be no cowards in this room."

No one else moves.

"Let's talk ideas, then. How can we hit them hard?"

"We should park a moving van with our logo on the side in front of their offices," Sasha says. "It will demoralize them."

The idea is so stupid that the silence that follows is painful. The CEO stares at her blankly.

"First, we should buy up all of the Google search results related to their name," I say. "We'll show up before they do on every search engine."

The CEO nods. "Keep going. That's a good start, but I want to do real damage."

"Targeted marketing campaign to their top clients," I say. "We send them something expensive—fancy wine, drones, rare cigars—and ask for a meeting."

"Excellent. Execute on that. Now I'd like to brainstorm around something illegal."

"Slash their car tires," Sasha says.

"No, not like that," the CEO says.

"We need a more sophisticated plan," Jeremy says.

"We need something unexpected. Something they aren't prepared for," I add.

The CEO looks at Corbett.

"Any ideas on your end?" he asks.

"Illegal, well, I just . . . I am not sure how much I know about illegal things," Corbett says. "We could plant drugs on them?"

"Let me take this offline with Sasha, Jeremy, and Cassie," the CEO says, nodding at me. "The team is decided. Everyone else is dismissed."

Corbett's face collapses and I glow from his failure. Jeremy cracks a rare smile. His pale cheeks remind me of the Alps, which

I have never seen except as a desktop screensaver. I think of them now, of mountain snow shining white in the sunlight.

In that flash of blinding white light, I can see my entire life: my calendar packed back to back with meetings; every hour, every minute, every second handed over to this CEO and his creation, his life's mission, not mine. I think of my bank account, my tiny overpriced apartment, the moment of my death, my last breath. Will any of this matter in the end?

Corbett leaves in a huff. With just the four of us sitting together, Jeremy runs a hand through his hair and the CEO takes a beat.

Outside, along the bay, men line the ground with fresh mulch for the purple flowers. The soil is a rich deep brown. I imagine standing up, walking out of the meeting and down to the flowers, lying beside them, stuffing handfuls of the new dirt into my mouth until my cheeks burst, tongue against damp earth, my face streaked with loam, the tide beside me rising and falling to the beat of my heart.

"What we need is a *strategy*," the CEO says. "That's what a war requires. They should think of my name whenever they hear the word *strategy*."

How many more hours of my life will I spend listening to men talk about themselves? I list my reliefs to calm myself:

- Masturbating

- The ocean at sunset

- A hot cup of ginger tea

- A line of cocaine from the bag in the freezer

- Sleeping in on Saturdays

"You're right," I say, filing away my mental list. "They've got to think of the word *strategy* whenever they hear your name."

"This is a war," Jeremy says. "We need to bomb them where it will hurt them most."

I list a century of wars: World War I, World War II, Korea, Vietnam, Afghanistan, Iraq. These were conflicts bathed in blood and vaporized by bombs. Our war consists of four people sitting around a conference room table.

"I picked you two because I know you can figure this out," the CEO says, nodding at Jeremy and me.

Sasha, Jeremy, and the CEO start outlining ideas: plans of attack, modes of sabotage, secret ways of spying. I speak up to offer two or three clear, concise ideas.

We eventually reach an impasse. Silence descends on the room. Then the CEO looks at me, directly into my eyes. My head swims. Despite my disdain, it is almost a holy experience to be acknowledged by him.

"What would a human do?" he asks. "How would a human handle this?"

The question hangs in the air. It takes effort to stop the grimace from crossing my face.

He has now shown his truest self. It's impossible to ignore what asking that suggests about the man. There are times when our words expose our reality.

"I simply mean," he says, "how would a human respond to this?"

I can't help but picture it: beneath his skin, streams of data, knots of colorful wires, all circuits and connectors, and in the center of his chest, a motherboard for a heart.

There is an air of forced restraint at the all-natural lunch buffet. Silver trays hold meat and steamed vegetables with salt-free seasoning. Sugar-free dessert is offered on Wednesdays only. Today is not Wednesday.

We fill our trays with the amount of food suggested by the portion sizes on the CEO's plate. Mine holds unseasoned chicken, carrots, lettuce with light dressing. They'll be looking. Plato believed that light emanated from the eyes. In these situations, I believe it: their eyes are on me, hot as searchlights.

Today my department has a team lunch in the big conference room. Our group is small and overworked. Sasha oversees everyone: a designer, a web developer, Corbett, me, an events coordinator, and a junior writer. I dread these lunches because anything can happen with Sasha.

"Let's play a game," she says through a mouthful of kale. She is wearing an oversized sweater and yoga leggings tucked into massive winter boots. Her hair is freshly dyed, and her mouth is freshly plumped. Red needle marks dot her lips.

"What kind of game?" Corbett asks.

"I was thinking we could play a new game called Tell Me," Sasha says. "I played it with my friends this weekend."

"Tell Me?" Corbett asks. "How do we play that?"

"Whoever starts says the phrase 'Tell me . . .' then asks whatever they want to know about everyone. That way we understand each other. It builds intimacy and trust. So I'll go first: *Tell me . . .* the most traumatic thing that has ever happened to you."

We shift our bodies around the table in noticeable discomfort. Then we remember how we're supposed to act.

"Love it!" the web developer says. "Let's play!"

"Absolutely," says the events coordinator. "I cannot wait."

"Are you in?" the writer asks, looking at me.

I cycle rapidly through my worst memories for an incident that will depict me as traumatized but not weak. I need something to hit just the right note: something forgettable enough that the team won't repeat the story but dramatic enough to satisfy Sasha.

"Sure," I say.

"I'll start," the web developer says. "My stepdad used to abuse my mom and that's why she left him. Your turn!"

"Okay, okay, wow, okay, so my ex-boyfriend died in a car accident when I was fifteen," the events coordinator says. "Just wow. It was awful. Okay, you go!"

"I am so sorry that happened to you. Thank you so much for sharing that with us," the writer says. "Okay, mine is kind of personal, but I had a lump removed from my breast."

She points to Corbett.

"Ahh, okay. Most traumatic. Let me think," Corbett says, his chin in his hand, staring up at the ceiling as if he is a great philosopher. "Well, I had a younger brother, but he died when he was born. I guess that's pretty traumatic."

All the eyes turn to me.

"I had spinal surgery and had to learn how to walk again," I lie.

"Wow, I am learning so much about all of you," Sasha says. "Okay, so once, back home in Russia, we had no water for many days and had to travel for miles to find a farm. Once we arrived there, my mother had to do something private with the farmer in order to get water from him. We took the water and went home and never spoke of it."

Everyone clucks in sympathy. The black hole is the size of a heart, levitating to the right in the periphery of my vision.

"Well, that was great," Sasha says. "I feel like we all truly understand each other in a new way. I've got to get going to a meeting."

"Me, too," the web developer says.

"Same," says Corbett. "It is an honor to be on this team."

"I can't wait to play this game again," the web developer says, beaming.

Everyone stands and begins to collect their plates of half-eaten food.

I wonder what in my life has led me to this moment, to this room, to this circle of people, all of our sorrows now suspended in the air. Our bodies have been split down the center, our guts spilled across the conference room table. And for what?

"By the way," Sasha says from the doorway, "I need you to come in at 3 a.m. tomorrow. We'll need a press release sent out abroad."

"But doesn't the PR team handle that?" I ask.

"Oh, I fired them this morning. They annoyed me."

"We need a PR team, don't we? I mean, at this stage of the company . . . I thought it was important?"

"Well, they're expensive. And you can do the work until you hire someone."

"Wait, who am I hiring?"

"You'll hire someone in Pakistan to handle PR. Have them work out of the Lahore office."

"Pakistan? Lahore office? What?"

"It's cheaper over there. Go get a young kid and pay them $25K. They'll think they're rich."

"I don't think this is a great idea."

"What do you know about PR? Nothing. I just need you to get through this press release and hire someone else."

"I just . . . paying someone in Pakistan less seems—" I say. "Isn't it . . . unethical to . . ."

"Are you against diversity? Don't you want a company with a rich array of ideas and minds?"

I bite my tongue. Every year, a diversity report on Silicon Valley's major players comes out. Last year, VOYAGER was in the bottom ten companies.

"Well, yeah, but it seems like we could find someone here and pay—"

She dismisses me with a wave. "I'll get the role approved by the CEO. Then you start interviewing. And I want that press release out tomorrow to all of our target countries. Don't fuck it up."

Salisbury steak

/ˈsȯlz-ˌber-ē- stāk/

noun

1. ground beef mixed with egg, milk, bread crumbs, and seasonings, and formed into a large patty and cooked.

e.g., Dinner on Thursdays was special when I was growing up: frozen Salisbury steaks with instant mashed potatoes.

"You do the potatoes," my mother said. "You always make them the best."

It was rare praise. I'd pour the off-white flakes into a bowl, add hot water and milk and garlic powder and sour cream. The extra ingredients made the fake potatoes seem real.

We ate dinner together most nights, the four of us around our little kitchen table. Usually it was cheap pasta with random vegetables. A portable television on top of the refrigerator glowed with the evening news. I set the table. I liked the exactness: four plates, four napkins, four forks, four knives, four glasses.

My little brother came down after my mother screamed up the stairs. He was dark eyed, dark haired, and tall. He collapsed his large frame into the chair next to mine.

"Hey," he said with a nod.

"Hey," I muttered.

My brother was a safe harbor from my parents. He kept a low profile, but sometimes we would sneak off and compare notes about our mother's latest insanity. I loved him in that silent way, the way where you don't even have to talk about it.

At the table, he used a big silver spoon to fish the Salisbury steak patties from their microwaveable container, where they were suspended in a sauce of brown sludge. Fake grill marks crossed the meat, three lines that made it look like my mother had done more than nuke the patties with the press of a button. He dropped a steak on my plate with a wet thud. The meat was glossy and soft beneath my fork.

My father kept the newspaper next to his plate for when he got tired of talking to us. My mother had the comics next to hers. My brother and I, we just sat there while they read. But first, my mother held her interrogations.

"So how was everyone's day?" she asked in a voice like a mother from television, an actress projecting across a studio. The sound made my throat tighten, the air constrict in my lungs.

"Good," I said. I tried to answer first in the hope of deflecting further questioning. It never worked.

"Well, good how?" she asked.

I held my day inside of me like a secret, a series of events I needed to protect. I had a mean teacher and a nice teacher and a crush and a few girls who were my friends. But I didn't want to tell her a thing. So instead I imagined a cloudless blue sky and I lied.

"I did a good job on an art project," I said. "I painted a mural of a Vincent van Gogh piece on the wall in the hallway."

"Wait, who?" she asked.

"Vincent van Gogh."

"Old famous dead art guy," my dad said. "Hacked off his ear. What a total freako."

"Yeah, that's him," I said.

"Well, okay," my mother said, her brow furrowed. She turned to my brother. "What about you?"

"I got a hundred on my math test," he said. His brown eyes flashed me an apology.

"There we go, something that makes goddamn sense," my mother said. "How about you, hon? How was the office?"

"Good, good," he said through a mouthful of meat. When he spoke, I could see the chewed gray lumps against his tongue. "Coming up on the end of the month, so you know how that is. Need to close a few big deals."

"You have some good leads?" my mother asked.

"Gonna try to close the two big whales, then get some little fishies," my dad said.

I knew about whales in nature: they lived in the ocean, toothed or toothless, singing their songs, a composition of moans and cries that could be heard for thousands of miles. I liked to think that I was singing that way, too, imperceptibly, beneath the surface of the dinner table.

"Whales at work?" I asked. "What does that mean?"

My father shoveled another forkful of glistening meat into his mouth before answering.

"Those are the big boys," he said. "They're the big companies that make for the biggest sales."

"Big as whales," my mom said. "That's get-a-new-car kind of money."

"Or pay-off-the-credit-card kind of money," my dad shot back. "Or get-the-car-inspected kind of money. Or save-up-for-her-college kind of money."

Money created a war zone in our house, and the credit card was a central area of conflict. The bill arrived at the beginning of the month and sparked a battle between my parents. My mother's secret purchases were revealed: a sweater for me, socks for my brother, a hideous ring from QVC with a synthetic sapphire in the center, perched on her finger, a lie you could only spot if you got close enough.

"This family can't survive on nothing," she said. "Everyone needs something sometimes."

It sounded like an old soul song.

"Everyone doesn't need everything all the time," my dad said. This time his mouth was empty, so the words were louder, sharper.

"We're not fucking poor! I won't live like we're fucking poor!" my mother shrieked. "I work too damn hard!"

"We're not rich, either!" my father yelled, pounding a fist on the table. The congealed brown sauce in the paper pan trembled as if in an earthquake. "You keep running around like we've got money to burn. Guess fucking what, princess? We don't!"

My brother and I kept our eyes trained on our plates. I traced the outline of the mystery meat. My face went red when they fought.

"You're a dick!" my mother shouted. "I didn't realize when we got married that I was marrying the king of dicks!"

"And I didn't realize I was marrying a moron who spent money like fucking water!" my father bellowed. "Guess what, princess? I'm turning the faucet fucking *off*!"

"I work, too," my mother shot back. "I should be able to spend money. You can't control everything."

"You can't control *anything*. That's why I have to do this! Otherwise you'd spend us into the poorhouse!"

My mother grabbed the comics and stood up with a force that shook the table again.

"Enjoy your dinner with this *dickhead*," she said, storming up the stairs.

My father took another bite of steak and slapped his newspaper back open.

"Nice fucking dinner," he muttered.

Then the room was quiet except for the television. My brother shrugged at me. There wasn't much to say. Besides, it was peaceful now, like a lake after a storm, flat and still as a mirror beneath the purple sky.

When I reach my limit, I do something the company frowns upon: I go outside alone. Taking time for yourself is seen as a betrayal, evading the great eye's surveillance. The great eye clocks my mood, my time management, my overall engagement and dedication.

Outside, I follow the perfectly landscaped path beneath the enormous palm trees by the bay. Gigantic California lilacs rising up purple and heavy on either side of me. The sky is wide and blue, with pure white clouds passing by slowly.

The scene seems perfect, but anxiety rears up in my chest, a thousand galloping red horses, my heart in my throat, my pulse in my ears. Images of my future failures flash by in a montage: alarm not going off, press release never sent, Sasha firing me in the big conference room, packing my life into boxes, everything collapsing before my eyes, starting all over again.

I stare out at the water. The black hole meets me at eye level and expands, growing to the size of a boat, then bigger than a house, then so big that I cannot see its edges, the force of it sucking at my skin. For a moment, I want to accept its invitation: step into the darkness, give myself over to its gravity.

Instead, I shake my head to break its hypnotic spell and pull out my phone.

"How's my daughter?" my father asks warmly after a few rings. The black hole shrinks beside me.

"I'm okay," I lie. "How are you?"

"Well, you'll be excited to know we've got a brand-new flavor of Oreo here. Putting those on the shelf. Are you ready for this?"

"I'm ready. What flavor are they?"

"Red. Fucking. Velvet."

"How incredible," I say. "I'm sure you'll be eating a hundred of those later."

"I do have that employee discount. And I think your mother will be excited. How's work?"

"Having one of those days. I don't know if I should have come here. They're asking me to do crazy shit again."

"You say that every few weeks, sweetheart."

"They ask me to do crazy shit every few weeks."

"I tell you this time and time again, sweetie. There's nothing back here for you. You couldn't have stayed. It was time for you to go."

As if everything simply vanished when I left. But there is still the town: the power plant stacks, the trees green in spring and fire red and orange in autumn, my parents' cars parked side by side in the driveway, the failed businesses with their bare windows and empty parking lots. There are still the people: the quiet addicts, the loud drunks, the woman down the street who was committed to a psychiatric facility, the man in the house opposite ours who hanged himself.

"I know, I know. I just . . . work is crazy, and I worry I'm fucking everything up."

"Everyone is fucking everything up all the time. All you can do is show up and try. This is how you get tough."

"I am, I am. You should see these people, though. It's scary. They don't exist for anything but this place."

"Well, you gotta remember that you're playing the game. You know, some people have no options. And you? You got options. Don't waste one worry on those fuckers. Worst case, you go work somewhere else."

"They are fuckers."

"I know, sweetheart, I know. They are honest-to-god fuckers. How's that gentleman you've been seeing?"

"I'm not really seeing him. It's . . . it's whatever."

"Well, how is it?"

"Fine . . . he's sweet."

"Getting-married sweet?"

"Get over it, Dad."

A voice comes over the store loudspeaker. "*Steve, we've got a restock on aisle five. Steve to aisle five.*"

"Well, I gotta get going. As you can hear, my services are in demand."

"Aren't you supposed to be retired? Why are you even doing this? You're supposed to be at home doing puzzles."

"Well, blame it on your mother. She ran up another secret credit card. Anyway, I don't mind it. There's a kid I work with who doesn't have a clue about the world. I have to teach him."

"Sure you do. Love you."

"Love you."

He hangs up. The silence after always hurts, as if I have lost something; no—as if something has been stolen. The black hole swells before me, mirroring the size of the constant ache inside of me. My chest heaves with a silent sob and a few tears gather in my eyes.

In the distance, I can see the tent dwellers tidying up their makeshift town.

My alarm goes off three times before I can pull my body from bed. It's dark outside. 2 a.m. I stumble through my routine, bleary, the black hole small beside me. I climb into a black car with tinted windows that drives me all the way to the office. There are only a few vehicles on the road, their lights blinding beams in the darkness.

The office is empty. It has a nice hollowness when it isn't filled with Believers. I carry a fresh cold brew to my desk and open Sasha's emailed feedback on my draft of a press release about VOYAGER's latest e-commerce report.

As I work, my fake self takes over: she churns through Sasha's final comments and edits, tweaking the ghostwritten quote from the CEO, updating the language to subtly underscore how terrible our competitor is, resolving the cold remarks on the copy along the way.

Once the press release is ready, I log into the PR portal and upload it for translation. Almost immediately, algorithms return the press release back to me in a dozen different languages I do not speak.

A map of the world appears on my screen. I click the countries far from here where we are relevant. Within minutes, the press release is out in the world, all over the globe, invisibly, the reach of the company ever expanding, an unstoppable force.

———

Four hours later, Sasha passes me on the way to her desk.
By now, I am delirious from lack of sleep and too much caffeine, both spent and keyed up.

"How did it go?" Sasha asks coldly.

"The press release?"

"Yes," Sasha says, rolling her eyes. "What else could I mean?"

"I made your final edits. It went out to every country you asked for at 3 a.m. our time."

"Just so you know, your draft of that press release was shit. The CEO would never talk like that."

"I updated it based on your feedback."

"I shouldn't have to give you feedback. You should be better at this. We hired you to be senior level."

A tremor shoots through my chest. For a moment, I fear she's going to fire me. Sweat breaks out under my arms and across my stomach. I pray it won't leak through my shirt, that she won't see how weak I am.

"I understand," I say. "I'm sorry."

"Don't say you're sorry. Just do better. And start interviewing for the Pakistan role. It's approved. Get a job posting up."

I turn back to my computer, where the PR portal shows the press release getting picked up by dozens of news outlets in other countries. It doesn't matter. It never will.

The job description opens with energetic lingo about the company culture.

Are you a motivated type A self-starter who is passionate and driven? At VOYAGER, we hire only the best. We're

looking for a top performer who is relentlessly in pursuit
of achieving our company goals. The ideal candidate will
have experience in public relations for a global company
and will dedicate themselves to quickly scaling awareness
of our brand in other countries. Working from our Lahore
office, the candidate will directly liaise with our marketing
team and CMO based in the epicenter of tech innovation,
Silicon Valley.

After a few tweaks, I post the listing on all the major global tech employment websites. Soon my inbox starts dinging. Within ten minutes, at least fifteen résumés are waiting for my review. I imagine fifteen hungry mouths chewing through the screen, clamoring for a chance to join the team.

The black hole hovers above my screen and widens. A new foreboding grows in my gut. Three more résumés arrive in my inbox. I shake my head at the void, unsure what I've done wrong.

Then I reread the job posting and it hits me: I used the exact same phrases from the job posting that tricked me into applying to VOYAGER a year ago. My inbox lights up again: six new résumés.

Notes & Research

- Albert Einstein's general theory of relativity introduced the concept of black holes alongside mapping out the links between space, time, and matter. However, even he was skeptical they existed in the real world.

- The term *black hole* was first used in December 1967 during a lecture by physicist John Wheeler. A student suggested the phrase as a replacement for a *gravitationally collapsed star*. Wheeler made the name stick.

- As new technology emerged, astronomers determined that black holes do exist; they evolved from numbers scrawled on a blackboard into reality.

- One of Stephen Hawking's greatest and most controversial findings: information that falls into a black hole gets destroyed and can never be retrieved.

- Hawking found any object that entered a black hole was not being spewed out before the black hole evaporated. Known as the Black Hole Information Paradox, Hawking's calculation meant black holes were destroying information that, according to quantum physics, could not be destroyed.

- "If determinism breaks down, we can't be sure of our past history, either," Hawking said of the theory. "The history books and our memories could just be illusions. It is the past that tells us who we are. Without it, we lose our identity."

mesocarp

/'mezəkärp/

noun

1. the middle layer of the wall of a ripened ovary or fruit.

2. often the fleshy part of a fruit, such as the edible part of a peach or the flesh that surrounds the seeds of a pomegranate.

The elevator is a metal tomb. There isn't enough air. I'm crammed inside with some Believers, including Corbett. Once a month, we cohost an event after work that brings "the greatest minds of the industry together" and features a roundtable with our CEO and the other CEOs of the Valley. It's an unspoken rule that attendance at these events is mandatory.

"Seems like you've been busy," Corbett says.

We both face the closed silver doors as the elevator climbs to the top of the building.

"Totally swamped," I say.

"Well, when you're relatively new and there's so much to learn, I can see why you'd be having trouble keeping up."

I refuse to look him in the eye, so I glare at his warped reflection in the elevator doors.

"I didn't say I was having trouble keeping up."

"Everyone struggles at first. I mean, I didn't, but technology comes naturally to me. I was born with a brain for it. I think most men are."

"I don't think that's how it works. Anyone can develop a skill. You don't need to be born with anything."

"You know, you should learn to code," he says. "It's very helpful in this industry. I think people who can code, especially women, are more respected and have a deeper understanding of our product."

I let the sentence die between us. The elevator doors finally slide open to reveal a fresh hell. Corbett smirks and is the first to step into the room.

"Looks great," he says. "I'm pumped for this."

Beyond his gigantic head, there is an open loft decorated in the partner company's signature electric purple. Posters with both company logos are mounted on every wall. Buckets of beer and boxes of pizza are arranged on long purple tables. Tall, bright refrigerators with clear doors are stocked with an exclusive flavor of kombucha brewed for the event.

"Holy shit," a man next to me whispers. "They got pizza."

He ambles toward the table in a daze.

My whole team is here: Corbett, the junior writer, and the rest of the marketing department. Their traumas still weigh on me, all of the pain they carry now somehow visible when I look at them. The forced intimacy has backfired since the lunch. Every single thing they do grates on me: the way they chew, their stupid comments, the way they actually want to be here working on a weeknight. I want to be at home, away from all of them. I want to forget their faces and their horrors.

Sasha wears her hair in a bun, a message to the world that she gets shit done. A bracelet on her arm reminds us with the phrase *Get Shit Done* in rose gold.

"No bullshit tonight," she says to me. "Transcribe everything the CEO says and then write a wrap-up for us to post tomorrow morning. I want this on the blog and I want more traffic. Your organic search numbers are down since yesterday."

"Organic search? We don't report those numbers until the team meeting next Monday morning."

"I've been keeping an eye on it, since it seems like you can't handle it."

"I can handle it."

"I can always hire someone to handle it. Someone with more experience."

I absorb the blow of her threat and force myself to nod. The room soon fills up with more anonymous faces, mostly a slew of the nameless young people who prop up the whole industry.

I find an empty table off to the right. On the purple stage, the CEO sits with three other CEOs. Sasha introduces them, then takes a seat on the side where she remains silent for the remainder of the event.

The CEOs wear blue button-downs with cuffed sleeves or sweaters with their company logos, paired with designer jeans, their wrists tricked out in the same smartwatch. They have frighteningly white teeth, clear eyes, and the smooth, calm foreheads of the wealthy.

The men speak with miniature flesh-toned microphones clinging to their cheeks. They talk about data, about privacy, about users, about monetization, gamification, synergy, strategy, onboarding, clicks, conversions, touchpoints. They are confident and clear, passionate and alive, the gods of the Believers, dedicated to the industry, to technology, to their missions.

I stare at them in horrified wonder as my fingers capture their words. I am a machine.

"What you want is to create a synergy so great that the user seamlessly converts," the CEO says. "But you want to accomplish this while utilizing data ethically, responsibly, mindfully."

Anger smolders beneath my skin. Precious hours of my life

are being lost to these men. More will be lost writing the wrap-up of the event when I get home.

Corbett stops by my table.

"Hope you're getting all of this," he says. "Don't fuck up his quotes this time. You got a few wrong in the last wrap-up. Nobody else noticed, but I did."

I don't respond, but inside I am a city ablaze, whole blocks burning, flames licking my rib cage, the inferno threatening to spill up my throat and from my mouth to devour the whole place.

After the event, my train home is delayed: a body has been found on the tracks. Men throw their bodies in front of the trains here, most often at sunset, the close of the business day. On weekday mornings, these men wake up, eat breakfast, and go to the office for the last time. I have yet to hear about a woman on the tracks.

When I finally board the late train, the evening sky is navy. I'm wrecked from the early morning press release, the event, and the remaining commute ahead of me. The body could be anywhere along the train route, deep in the Valley or up north, closer to the city.

The train car is full of men, men still in the business of living, still in the business of technology. I hear them taking calls, whispering to their colleagues and wives, saying, "Will it scale?" and, "I'll be home late."

Each time it happens, I can't help but envision the bodies: shredded by the velocity and sheer mass of the trains, their blood seeping under the tracks and into the earth. I wonder what their last thoughts were.

I peer into the aisle and notice the girl from sales a few feet away from me. Her face is wet, and I realize she is quietly sobbing. I imagine another scene: I walk up to her and extend my friendship, offer support. But she turns her head and our eyes meet. She stares right through me, as if she has never seen me before.

My ovaries cramp and my eyes almost water from the pain. I have no one to talk to about what might be happening inside of me. The black hole floats beside me, hovering near my stomach, almost protective.

I can't help but picture a faceless man on the train tracks, split open, his innards glistening under the station lights. I can't help but picture myself on the tracks, halved, all my insides glistening, too, all of my problems solved.

technology

/tekˈnäləjē/

noun

1. the application of scientific knowledge for practical purposes, especially in industry.
2. machinery and equipment developed from the application of scientific knowledge.
3. the branch of knowledge dealing with engineering or applied sciences.

e.g., It is not clear who decided what color the Internet should be, but it is considered to be blue. Certainly, black and white are integral, but the overwhelming blueness is astounding. There is a reason for the hue: blue, like the sky and the sea, is proven to relieve mental anguish. Blue is the color of serenity, piety, sincerity, and the hue tricks us, pulls us back to our screens, again and again. We are drawn to that new blue, the blue of a wide manufactured sky, an endless, false sea. But what happens when we move away from the soft glow of the screens, away from the pixelated serenity?

e.g., I was fourteen when the first computer entered our home.

"We can't afford this," my father said.

"Too late," said my mother.

It was a big beige box. My father cursed at the strange new

cables as he set it up. We heard a phonelike sound. Then we were online.

"One hour per day," my mother said. "That's it."

The screen was a new portal to enter. I created online profiles with song lyrics and searched for poetry and horoscopes, watched videos and messaged friends. Whenever I went online, the black hole hovered over my shoulder, a lone spying eye.

Soon I became addicted: I'd sneak down to the computer in the middle of the night. My heart would pound as the dial-up modem connected, which I'd cover with a blanket to muffle the sound. I'd message my friends and sometimes random men in chat rooms.

"What the fuck are you doing?" my mother said when she caught me. There were punishments: no snacks, no television, no Internet.

But I'd find a way back to the screens. I always did. I was already a different person. My brain shifted, rewired itself, made space for the new blue glow.

There is a knock, his knock, and I open my front door. His dark eyes sparkle above his thick brown beard. He wears a crisp white button-down, jeans, and recently shined boots.

It is, finally, Friday. I've showered and lined my nose with powder. The black hole is a pinprick.

The chef has a girlfriend, but she doesn't have anything to do with us. We have no label, and without the pressure of one, a thin slit becomes an opening through which a certain type of love can emerge. A love like ours requires special conditions, the way certain flowers only bloom at night beneath a full moon.

"There she is," he says.

"You're on time."

"Always. I made these for you today."

He hands me a small brown box and I open the lid. Inside: two small frosted doughnuts, each decorated with pale pink flowers and tiny red strawberries.

"They're lovely," I say.

He takes me up into his arms right there in the doorway. When we kiss, it is like a symphony, our mouths moving in unison, sure of the other's next move. Biting lips, caressing cheeks, pulling hair, his hands finding my bottom beneath the hem of my dress. Here in the doorway, nothing else exists.

"Would you like some wine?" I ask when we break apart.

"You taste a little strange tonight," he says, touching his lips.

I realize he can taste the drugs on me and look away.

"Wine?" I repeat.

"Of course. Red?"

"You know it."

I place the doughnuts on the counter and pour him a glass. We move to the couch and I drape my legs across his lap.

"How was your day?" I ask.

"Nuts. We were slammed. But everything's prepped for tomorrow night's big dinner. Our whole menu is color focused."

"Color?"

"Each plate features a different color. The appetizer is green, the first course is yellow, second course is blue. Dessert is black. Oh, you'd love that one. Let me show you."

He pulls out his phone. I glance at the photo on the screen and my stomach drops. On the plate is a round black mirror.

"It's a black hole," he explains. "You see that shine? I use a chocolate and coconut charcoal mirror glaze. It's impossible to do it justice in a photograph, but I'm really into how the dish turned out."

"It's beautiful," I say, pushing the words over a new lump in my throat. I drink my wine to drown the dark feelings rising. The black hole swells along with the emotions briefly, as if threatened, then shrinks back down.

"How about your day?" His hand finds my bare thigh, and one finger slides beneath my dress, marking an electric path over my skin.

"Meetings, meetings, meetings," I say.

"Big boss lady," he teases.

"Not exactly."

"Soon enough, you will be."

"Do you want to watch the octopus?"

"Yes, please."

I click on the television and cue up the nature series we both love. A British man narrates as a gigantic octopus moves along the ocean floor. The octopus is vulnerable out in the open. Tentacles extended, she gathers shells and pulls them to her. She uses the suckers on her arms to arrange the shells against her body, until she is camouflaged. An eel weaves dangerously close to her but passes by, oblivious.

"The octopus has three hearts," I say.

"I know," he says. "So does the cuttlefish."

"They're iridescent."

My mind flicks through other iridescences: soap bubbles, butterfly wings, seashells, bismuth, stag beetles, peacock feathers, muscle, labradorite, clouds, compact discs, oil on asphalt after a rain, my blood on cocaine.

"Not exactly. But they do look that way."

His hand moves further up my dress. His fingers curve around my upper thigh. Our mouths meet again, and he slides me down onto the couch cushions. I wrap my legs around him and his hand finds my breast. The scene plays out the same every time: our bodies press against each other through our clothes until he stands and pulls me to my feet. I click off the television, turning the blue sea black.

He leads me to my bedroom, and we find each other's bodies again on the bed. What happens next is private. A red curtain descends on the scene. But behind the curtain, what we have is explosive, exquisite, symphonic. When we both moan, we do so as a single bell, golden and ringing out through the velvet of the night.

intimacy

/ˈin(t)əməsē/

noun

1. close familiarity or friendship; closeness.
2. a private, cozy atmosphere.
3. an intimate act, especially sexual intercourse.

e.g., I'd gone to a restaurant with only the black hole for company. It levitated above the empty seat to my left at the long counter. It was one of those open-air affairs, where you could watch the kitchen like the inside of a clock, the metal gears turning. He was wearing one of those expensive aprons you see in magazine profiles of top chefs.

But I didn't care about that. I cared about the way he ran the kitchen. Everyone called him Chef with a reverence I had never heard before. The way he held his power was graceful: he was quiet and thoughtful with the staff, but there was an intensity behind it all, a fire.

We caught eyes over my main course, a handmade pasta. Our eyes lingered for a beat too long. He turned back to running the kitchen, with renewed gusto, a little louder, so I could hear what had before been low calls to his crew.

Plates I hadn't ordered began to appear in front of me: a small forest made of mushrooms, a bite of braised Wellington in the shape of a snail, a plate of pastry swans stuffed with cheese and swimming in a pond of red wine.

For dessert: a white chocolate truffle suspended in a stretch of spun sugar that looked to be rocketing up from the plate.

"It's a comet," he said quietly from over my right shoulder.

He took the seat to my right. The closeness of him was dizzying. Already, I felt a heat between us. The black hole spun and buzzed on the other side of me. But I ignored it.

We found each other's eyes and held each other there again. It wasn't the look of lust. That was inside of the look, yes, but it was wrapped in a rare softness—an immediate recognition.

"Every plate has been absolutely beautiful," I said. "It's like art."

"I liked watching you eat them," he said. "I liked surprising you."

"How do I eat this comet?" I asked, suddenly shy.

"You'll want to start with the tail," he said softly.

He moved his hands, slowly, carefully, to break off the long delicate stretch of crystalline sugar.

"Then you'll want to eat the truffle," he said. His voice was syrupy.

I slid the truffle into my mouth and bit: an explosion, not too sweet, a different note than I was expecting, laced with the lightness of mint. I closed my eyes and let it dissolve on my tongue.

"Good?" he asked.

"Like eating a star," I said.

Our bodies moved closer. We continued speaking in low tones, until the kitchen shut down, until everyone went home. He brought down bottles of wine, and we whispered about who we were, where we were from, what we wanted, our secrets.

Eventually, his hand found my thigh beneath the table. We didn't sleep together that night, but his mouth did find mine, later, out on the street, and the kiss felt like two galaxies colliding.

e.g., It didn't stop there. There were more dates. Every two or three days, we would find each other for dinner. He took me to secret bars beneath other bars, entering with a password. He took me to a restaurant with a lake inside, where a band played on the water. He took me to sample a private chef's tasting menu, where each bite was assembled by hand.

At these dinners, our hands roved over each other's legs under the table. I'd reach up and touch his neck. He'd run his finger along the inside of my elbow, press down on my pulse. Each night ended with our mouths together. We kissed like art, like water, like there was an endless clear stream between us.

When we were together, the black hole stayed small. Our connection was big enough to shrink it, keep it contained.

On our sixth date, at dinner, his hand found its home on my leg.

"I need to talk to you about something," he said. His eyes looked frantic; he was almost wincing.

"Hm?" I said, my mouth full of pasta and egg yolk and cheese.

"I should have told you the night we met."

I swallowed. My anxiety spiked. I waited for it, the confession: he was married with children, a felon, a sex trafficker. The black hole swelled to the size of a melon. It began to sing its song.

"Well . . . I don't know how to say this," he said. "I've never had to tell anyone this before. But I'm in an open relationship. We have an apartment together."

An invisible fist punched me in the chest, rattling my heart.

"Oh," I said.

The black hole expanded and began to vibrate.

"All of this is new for me," he said. "I don't know how to handle it, to be honest. You're the first . . . you're the first person I've actually dated since we opened the relationship."

Open. I felt as though I might throw up. Somewhere in the city, a faceless woman waited for him at home. She was a threat from afar, able to descend on me whenever the urge struck.

"She wants to explore things with women, certain things I cannot give her," he said. "We're very honest with each other, brutally honest."

Jealousy reared up in my chest at a series of scenes my mind created of him with this woman: mornings in bed together, drinking coffee in the kitchen, him with his arm wrapped around her waist. A woman with an eyeless swirling whorl for a face perched on a lithe body with perfect breasts. I hated the thought of their intimacy.

"She knows I have feelings for you. And my relationship with her doesn't have anything to do with how we are together. You are singular to me."

I have known sadness my entire life. I recognized the message: I would never have anything, not in a real way. The best I could do was the discount version.

"Okay," I said. "What are the . . . I mean, are there rules?"

"The one rule we have is that I can't fall in love with you," he said. "I can only like you very much. And I do. I like you very, very much."

An invisible wall was built between us in that moment, a boundary we couldn't move beyond, the place where the fantasy broke down and reality took over.

I didn't want it, didn't want any of it, didn't want to share him. I wanted all of the borders between us to dissolve, I wanted us to blur into each other, I wanted the deep red of our hearts to touch.

But all of my language was caught hot in my throat, burning. I was choking on what I wanted, on how to tell him. And beyond what I knew I wanted was another desperate desire, one deeply ingrained in me, a need encoded in every single one of my cells: I didn't want him to leave.

There are moments in which a certain level of pain is chosen in order to avoid another, deeper pain. I leaned over and kissed him with a deliberate hunger, desperate to prove nothing had changed between us. I didn't want the mirage to disappear.

The black hole hovered above him and expanded, as if threatening to swallow him whole. It hissed a furious warning. But I knew it couldn't help me.

The amount of pain we can endure is spectacular. We are conditioned to withstand torture, to haul gray boulders of hurt on our shoulders, to confront the pressure endlessly, the heavy rough stone wearing away at us until our skin breaks open, revealing the bloody red flesh below.

As always, I wake to the ghost of the chef: his scent on the sheets and a dent on a pillow. It is almost as if he is an event that never happened, a timeline I never lived, just a love I experienced during a dream.

The black hole looms near the ceiling, big and spinning slowly. I look up into its depths and try, once again, to understand where it leads. Then a hypnotizing glint of red heat deep in its darkness winks at me.

There is a familiar crack in my chest, near my heart, and the sharp ache of loneliness returns, the reality of being unknown, never truly known, by anyone in the world. The sensation seems endless, a dark sky that extends into a universe that extends into yet another universe and then another beyond that, a horizon with no final point.

The sound of a beeping trash truck breaks me out of the reverie. I can hear metal against metal, then garbage and glass crashing against itself. I remember I have to bring dessert to a dinner party.

Most of my new friends have lived here for years or even decades, in rent-controlled apartments with tall windows that invite in the unreliable sunlight.

"You need to get a cheaper apartment," they advise. "There's a spot open in a house with three other people about thirty minutes away."

I can't stand the thought of living with three roommates, my privacy gone. We discuss money here openly, sharing how we manage to stay afloat above the rising cost of living.

"I got this apartment for a steal. Twenty-five hundred dollars a month," my fake self says.

"That's unheard of," my friends say. "Rents like that don't exist anymore."

And it's true they don't. My rent is three thousand dollars a month. But my fake self always knocks the price down.

Here is the truth: I am balancing on a tightrope, high in the air, no net. After taxes, there isn't enough money. My paychecks evaporate to rent and student loan payments. My savings account has dwindled since I moved.

Accounts
Checking: $220
Savings: $550

Here is another truth: I shop at the discount Grocery Outlet a neighborhood over.

Outside, the city is full of eyes: the sidewalks and the buildings and the very air are made up of people looking at me. Each step I take feels monitored, as if everyone and everything is judging me by my parts: thighs, flanks, breasts, hair, outfit, shoes, purse. If it isn't the great eye of the company or the black hole watching my every move, then it is the eyes of the city.

Everything here is always in bloom, even in winter. The heads of dark pink flowers slowly explode in the sun like bursting hearts. I walk past graffiti flowers and foxes, boutique art stores, homeopathic centers, food stands, and a Buddhist temple housed in an old Gothic church. The doors to the temple are open. A glimpse inside: a black floor, intricate gilded columns rising to the ceiling, bald men in red robes praying at a gigantic altar. Seeing their faith is like peering into another way of living, their prayer a portal to a peace I have never found.

Past the post office, past the fruit stand, past the fish store with its rows of silvery bodies on ice is the outlet. The store has a big red sign and looks like any other grocery, except it's a little run down. This is the only place in the city where I feel rich. A rush of purchasing power floods my brain when I step inside, and I give myself over to the tide.

I cruise the fluorescent aisles: expired fancy cheeses, chicken breasts right on the edge of their best-by date, dented cans, two-packs of off-brand pink razors, discounted sweatpants, fancy candles with broken wicks, cheap kitchen accessories, rejected protein powder flavors.

In the dessert section, I scan the display: almost-stale croissants, questionable chocolate rugelach, sugar cookies with machined slabs of pink icing. My eyes land on a perfectly round vanilla cake with no apparent flaws. I move quickly and carefully, placing it in my basket before anyone else lunges for it.

In the checkout lane, a popular sad song plays over the store speakers. The same feeling I had on the train comes back to me, the premonition that this might be the moment that will change everything.

But nothing meaningful happens. The cashier takes my

payment, slides the cake into a bag. I return home the way I came, back through bright murals and shit, food carts and graffiti, as young men flash by on green electric scooters, laughing at a joke I didn't hear.

Back at my apartment, it happens again. In the silence of my living room, my anxiety balloons and the black hole expands in response.

Below my window, the people who sleep on the streets are gone. In the weekend daylight, it's another city entirely. People chat with friends, stroll hand in hand with their lovers, buy armfuls of flowers. Everyone else seems to know what to do with their free time: shopping, getting high on a blanket at the park, going to yoga, slacklining between palm trees. I can hear the fullness of other lives through the window, a party I wasn't invited to, a distant parade.

I do nothing. I sit on the sofa, paralyzed by my own mind, my apartment walls a coffin. The black hole gets closer, opens wider, blotting out most of the living room.

As the scent of fruit and metal overwhelms me, my mind devolves into terrified paranoia: *I am going to get fired, I am pregnant, I am going to hit rock bottom, I am going to lose everything.*

outer horizon

/ˈoʊdər həˈrīzən/

noun

1. The outer horizon is the event horizon of the
   black hole in the usual sense of the term.
2. The outer horizon is the boundary of the region
   from which null curves (the paths of light rays)
   do not escape to infinity.

e.g., There are two types of black holes: a nonrotating black hole
is known as a Schwarzschild black hole, while a rotating black
hole is known as a Kerr black hole.

In a Kerr black hole, like mine, the outer horizon is important:
if you go beyond the ergosphere and fall past the outer horizon,
there is no returning. Just like the paths of light rays, you would
no longer be able to escape.

e.g., There are moments in life that are points of no return: we
make a single choice and our futures are determined. It might not
even be a choice. You might be forced beyond the outer horizon
with no chance of escape. There might be no other option.

e.g., My father sat me down at the kitchen table late one day
in my senior year of high school. My mother was cleaning the

bathroom, her hands in yellow rubber gloves, the burn of bleach wafting through the house.

"We need to talk," my father said, a white envelope spilling out onto the table, a piece of paper from my school telling him the truth of me.

"Yeah?"

"You failed math and science." His voice was serious, edging on the way he spoke when he was going to smack me across the face. "Your mother is furious. And I'm disappointed. Do you want to tell me what the fuck that's about?"

"*Furious,*" my mother shouted from the bathroom.

"*I told you I was handling it,*" my father bellowed.

My face flushed. I imagined what would happen: failing high school, unable to get a good job, stuck in this town.

"Now listen," he said. "You're going to go to summer school. They'll let you walk in graduation and then you'll make this up. But you're going to get rid of that shitty boyfriend, stop smoking, and get your fucking act together. Understood?"

"I understand," I said, panic thrumming through me. The boyfriend was bad: long brown hair, a permanent cigarette lit between his forefingers, a white Camaro convertible that he frequently used to steal me away from my parents.

"This boyfriend, failing these classes," my father said. "Work your shit out and go to college. Because once you graduate, this isn't your home anymore. The train is leaving the station."

"What train?"

"The train of fucking life, sweetheart. And your ass better be on it."

I nodded. I imagined the train of life rushing toward me. It would either run me over or I'd find a way to board.

———

e.g., After a blur of summer school, I landed at a state school situated in a valley four hours from my parents' house. I'd placed into the English program on the strength of my essay alone. The valley was known for keeping its population isolated, distant from big cities and outside news. It was a place of safety and fantasy, a self-contained universe.

"Now you're on the train," my father said the night before I left home. "But let me make one thing clear: we will help pay for some of your college, but you have to keep your grades up. Otherwise, we won't be here to help."

I pictured myself on a series of trains, all of which moved like lightning across the land, horns blaring, the scenery whipping past before I could register what I was seeing as they took me far away from home, into a new life.

"I want to stay on the train," I said, not entirely sure what I was agreeing to other than moving out and not coming back.

e.g., In front of the bland concrete of the dorms, I tested my legs like a newborn calf. I wobbled away from the watchful eyes of my parents, away from our townhouse and the power plants and the ex-boyfriend.

With the black hole leashed to me, I made friends and went to concerts, I studied, I took tests, I read, and I wrote. I tried to shake off the weight of my hometown, of my upbringing, of my family, despite the phone calls that sucked me back, pulled at me like tentacles, their voices curling around my ear.

Throughout it all, the sadness continued. I learned to recognize its rhythm by the way the black hole reacted. I drank heavily to make it shrink, but each morning I woke alone, it hovered above my hungover head.

Graduation loomed, and with it the expectation that I would become an adult. And then there I was, in a blue cap and gown, on an arena stage. There I was, walking across it, my parents cheering from the stands, and then there I was with a diploma in my hand and a new life unfolding before my eyes again.

"There's another train pulling up," my father said. "And it's leaving the station. And your ass better be on it."

"Which train is it this time?" I asked.

"It's the fucking job train," he said. "Because listen up, buttercup, you can go anywhere you'd like, but you're sure as hell not moving in with us ever again."

e.g., And then it began: the flurry of job applications, the interviews, the first day at work in an office in the big city forty minutes from my parents' house, a new life built in a Philadelphia row home with four roommates, each one of them an artist or a musician.

I didn't know it then, but the cycle would continue for years: job after monotonous job, title after title, commuting back and forth on an endless highway, promotions and small bonuses, two weeks' vacation, slowly losing motivation with each job, the black hole never far away.

But for a moment, before the first job, the bright light of an escape hatch flashed before me. In those early days, I believed that there was another way to live and I just had to figure out what it was.

Isn't that always the way adult life begins? You think you'll become something different, something new. At first, you swim violently against the tide, your body straining until your muscles give out, until you can't push any harder, until you stop fighting and float, letting the water take you back to shore, where the rest of the world is already at the office, typing on their computers beneath buzzing fluorescent lights, toiling away in the glare of permanent productive daylight.

The sunshine is frigid despite its bright glare. My shoulders shiver as I walk in a thin dress. I've forgotten a jacket again, still not adjusted to the bright, cold curse of San Francisco winter. The dinner party is two neighborhoods over, and I have to pick up my friend Maria on the way. I carry the cake with my arm bent, so I don't ruin the perfect ribbons of white frosting.

The melancholy from earlier continues, unrelenting, wave after wave of sorrow crashing against my ribs. I don't want to go to this dinner—groups of people make me feel too exposed, I never know what to say, I always drink too much and make a fool of myself. At the same time, I cannot go anywhere else but the dinner party. At least while I'm there, the black hole will shrink to the size of a small beast I can bear. If I'm alone tonight, it will widen and sing its eternal song until I lose my mind.

"I'm having a panic attack," Maria says, stepping from her doorway into the street. She reaches up and tugs at one of her curls. That's how her anxiety manifests: she pulls at a spring in her hair without thinking.

Maria: Black, with brown hair and big brown eyes gone watery from stress. She has panic attacks regularly. She can't tell me what triggers them due to an NDA she signed that swears her to silence about every aspect of her job. I never know how to comfort her because I never know exactly why she's upset.

"Fuck them!" she shrieks on the sidewalk, stomping her foot. Then she looks over both shoulders. "Do you think someone heard that? My coworkers live around here. Did you see any of them? Do you think they'll report me to my company?"

"I don't think anyone heard you," I say.

"My last panic attack lasted twenty hours. I was paralyzed on the floor and the damn dog kept licking my face. It was funny, in a way."

Maria has a droopy dog and a Xanax prescription. On walks, the dog's absurdly long ears trail on the sidewalk.

Panic attacks were a mystery to me before San Francisco. But soon, it was my body on the light gray tile in the bathroom, my heart clawing at my ribs as if it had arms. I couldn't breathe, and I saw a very bright light, which is what I assume dying must be like. I understand Maria deeply in this way.

"I'm sorry," I say. "This city is a fucking nightmare."

"I saw a man set himself on fire in front of my morning coffee spot a few weeks ago."

"I saw a man on fire a few days ago, too," I say. "But it was at night."

We keep a running list of the city's latest horrors: a pigeon with no feet eating vomit, a pantsless man shitting on the sidewalk in broad daylight, a woman screaming in conversation with herself, another woman blacked out on the street before sunrise beneath the tender wet trees, her feet bleeding red through her white cotton socks in the rain.

This last scene sent me into a profound depression for a long stretch of days. With each horror, a new slit is cut into my brain. The way wild amounts of wealth brush up against extreme poverty and displacement here is like nothing I've ever seen. Maria and I are somewhere in the middle: neither wealthy nor displaced, just suspended in the air, writhing, having our little panic attacks.

"You brought dessert?" she says, gesturing at the bag.

"Yeah, what did you bring?"

She hefts the plastic bags in her hands.

"Five bottles of wine. Four for us, one for them. Do you want a Xanax?"

I laugh up into the cold sun.

"Yeah, fuck it," I say. "How else am I going to get through this dinner?"

I place the white pill on my tongue and swallow it. When the Xanax enters my bloodstream, I will experience something close to bliss: the black hole will be subdued for a few hours.

"Hell yeah, girl," Maria says. "We do it dry sometimes. That's how we live."

It is too soon to be true, but I feel calmer already.

friendship

/ˈfren(d)ship/

noun

1. the emotions or conduct of friends; the state of being friends.
2. a relationship between friends.
3. a state of mutual trust and support between allied nations.

e.g., I wasn't good at keeping friends. Once in a while, I would call a casual friend back home and lie about how perfect San Francisco was.

But usually whenever I was alone, the black hole warped the time and space of my life: hours would pass before I realized I had only been sitting on the sofa, gazing into its abyss.

e.g., My friendship with Maria is based on convenience and a shared hatred of San Francisco. She lives a few blocks away above a gourmet bone broth store. I met her one day at Dolores Park when I was sitting alone on a bench.

"Do you hate it here as much as I do?" she called from a blanket on the grass. I could tell immediately she wasn't a Believer.

"I guess I do," I said.

She stood up and made her way to me, pulling two cans of

beer from her gigantic jacket pockets. After that, we were in it together.

We spilled our stories. She spent three years working as a contractor for one of the biggest tech companies in the Valley, flying from Miami to SF and back, until they brought her on full-time.

"I'm a fucking diversity hire," she told me over our cans of beer. "You should see all these assholes patting themselves on the back for having me there."

I didn't know how to argue with her. Tech companies calculate diversity numbers to hit, and once there is a number, they achieve it like any other metric.

Maria and I made short lists of other cities we'd move to. We brought them up on first dates with men from the apps: *Where will you go after this?* We hummed the lists to ourselves like lullabies.

I had turned my words over in my head until they were smooth stones: *Austin, Atlanta, Bordeaux, Lisbon, Philadelphia.* Maria's list is different, and includes her ex-boyfriend, Marco: *Miami, Marco, Atlanta, Marco, Oaxaca, Marco.*

e.g., A few weeks later, Maria's company hosted an event at an elite private club. The club was a labyrinth of art, bands, bars, and rooms with secret entrances.

We were doing shots when Nicole walked up. She wore an expensive dress and was of an indeterminable age, but she had more wrinkles around her eyes than we did.

"You two look fun," she said.

"The most fun here!" I said, drunk.

"More fun than the rest of these clowns!" Maria agreed.

"Is this your first time here? I'm Nicole. I head up publicity for the club," she said.

"First time, and this place is wild," I said. "Can't tell if I love it or hate it."

"You love it. Let me show you something."

She led us to a bookshelf and pulled on a small golden globe. The entire shelf slid to the left, revealing a secret room: bright green walls and black leather chairs with a record player in the center of a golden table.

"Have fun," she said. "I'll check back in on you two later."

She returned with a small tray of shots and we drank until well after midnight. After that, we were friends with Nicole, out of a combination of loneliness and necessity. She invited us to the club regularly. Certain friendships are built on a mutual love and understanding. Other friendships are built on the upsides.

The dinner party I dread is at Nicole's house. We knock on her front door and wait.

A small panic runs through me at the thought of a night with Nicole. She's fine overall, though there are moments when she turns completely psychotic. A seemingly innocuous exchange might upset her, triggering a volcano of screaming and smashing. She's never been violent toward me, but her anger is so wild that the possibility hangs in the air.

Just then the Xanax kicks in, making me soft, transparent, a woman made of water vapor. The sweet chemical calmness relaxes every nerve in my body. My neck muscles loosen, and my shoulders pull themselves away from my ears. I am deeply at ease with the universe and my place in the order of things. The black hole behind me shrivels into a pinprick, a distant star.

The door swings open. Nicole stands before us: pale, brunette, dark eyes, zaftig in a black caftan.

"My loves!" she says with a manic grin.

"Nicole!" I say back.

"Hey, girl," Maria mutters, tugging at her curls.

"Come in, come in! Dinner is almost ready. Oh, oh, oh, take your shoes off, yes, right there, right by the door. Oh, oh, what did you bring there? Is this a cake? Oh, how lovely! And, Maria! So much wine! Everyone! Everyone! They're here!"

Three women I haven't met before sit around the small table in Nicole's kitchen. The stove is full of covered pots, and a few lit candles dot the scene. Nicole's fat tortoiseshell cat emerges from its litter box in the nearby bathroom. The faint scent of cat shit wafts over the smell of dinner to greet me.

"Hey, everyone," I say.

"Hey, girls," Maria says. "What's up?"

The women are all skin pulled taut over bone, all puffy vests, tanned flesh, honeyed highlights. The puffy vests are a constant here and a signifier: most start-ups give their employees a puffy vest after four years of service. The women introduce themselves. They are named Cat or Diane or Liz or Leslie. My brain won't hold this information. They resume their conversation.

"And so I said to Jared, you know, if we're going to drink this much green juice, the industrial juicer will pay for itself in, like, three weeks."

"You're totally right. He'd be a fool not to see that."

They keep talking: new succulents, hot yoga class, stock options, making their own kombucha and yogurt. Usually I would sit in sullen rage and spend the night shooting eye daggers across the table at them. But in the drugged country of my newly softened heart, I can graciously accept their lives.

At the kitchen counter, Nicole pulls the cake from the bag.

"Gorgeous, gorgeous," she says to no one as she lifts the cake from the box and places it on a brown-and-orange speckled plate. The cake now looks like a bad painting at MoMA.

"What's for dinner?" I ask, my mouth moving a beat too slow.

"Oh! Well, I made my famous lasagna and we need to prep a little salad! You know how I love a little salad! Help me chop the veggies?"

She hands me a glass of wine and steers me to a small cutting board covered with cherry tomatoes. A glinting knife sits next to the board.

"Get to *work*, honey," she singsongs.

I take a gulp of wine and swear I can feel it staining my teeth. That's how in tune I am with my body thanks to the Xanax. I grab the knife and a small tomato, slicing directly into the center. Seeds and juice squirt onto the cutting board. I keep going, halving the sections, like a surgeon. I laugh at the idea: a doctor, dull kitchen knife in hand, removing tumors from sick patients.

"What's so funny?" Nicole demands, a flash of her darkness rising to the surface.

"Oh, I was pretending I was a surgeon," I explain, but my mouth moves a beat too slowly again.

"Are you high?"

"What? No! I was just having fun. It's a fun time! It's a dinner party. Par-tay time."

"I hate it when you show up this high. You know I do. I'm fine with weed, but I asked you not to do harder drugs around me. I wish you could just respect me."

I roll my eyes up to the roof of my skull. She can't see my face, but it feels good.

"I know you're rolling your eyes, you stoned asshole. Don't fuck up my dinner party."

I am so high that I let her say it without any fuss.

Our knees bump beneath the small dinner table, which is crowded with our plates, the giant slab of red lasagna, and the bowl of salad. The whole display is domestic, civilized, almost a scene from a heartwarming sitcom about a group of female friends.

I take another sip of wine. Maria's eyes are glassy. She looks as if she might fall into her plate. I step on her foot under the table and she straightens up.

"Okay, okay, damn," she mutters. "You don't have to be a bitch about it."

"So, ladies! Catch me up on your lives," Nicole says as she slides a knife into the red lasagna.

A pair of hands passes me the salad bowl, and I slap some lettuce and bits of red tumor onto my plate.

"Well, Brad took me up to Point Reyes last weekend," says a girl with mousy brown hair wearing a puffy red vest. "We had the best cheese. It was so *cute*."

"Oh my god! It's amazing there! How romantic!"

"Tell me about it. Brie really sets the mood!"

Maria catches my eye across the table. She makes a finger gun and holds it to the side of her head. I let out a sharp laugh. The Xanax has taken over more of me and I'm no longer sure why we came here. Nicole kicks me under the table.

"Okay, now you go, Maria!" Nicole says.

"Uhhh, well," Maria says. "I'm working on a project I can't talk about. But it's super intense and it will probably change the world."

"As usual! She's too important to tell us anything. What about you?" Nicole asks, directing her interrogation at me. "What's going on with you?"

"Oh, you know, work is crazy," I say. "Nothing else is going on, really."

"What about that guy? The chef?" she asks.

The red door of my heart slams shut. I don't want these women to know anything about my private life.

"He's fine," I say.

"Well, give us the details for god's sake! Are you in love?"

"I wouldn't say that. He does bring me handmade doughnuts every Friday."

"He does what?" Nicole shrieks.

"Oh my god, so romantic," one of the faceless women says.

"The most romantic," Maria says, making no effort to hide her sarcasm. "I wonder what he does for his girlfriend."

Something snaps inside of me. Maybe it's the pill, or maybe it's from the torture of staring at their stupid faces and their puffy vests. I decide, for the remainder of the evening, to become one of them.

"Yes, it's *so* romantic," I say. My fake self takes over and I am a woman on a stage: glowing, successful, satisfied, centered, chakras aligned. "We're so cute, it's kind of gross? He's going to take me for oysters."

I let myself blush as they coo over me, the Xanax and wine working in harmony, and I feel, for once, normal. I feel like the three women whose names I don't know. We chat like old friends before I ruin it.

"What do you all think about the virus?" I blurt out.

The table goes silent.

"I mean . . . it's not here so what's the point?" says one of the girls.

"Yeah, I mean, it's an abroad thing," Nicole says, shrugging, then stuffing lasagna into her mouth. "Anyway, California is different. I keep telling you that. Besides, they always make this shit up. Remember Ebola? Whatever happened to that?"

"Right, right," I say.

"Anyway, don't ruin dinner over it," Nicole says.

Once again, I've said the wrong thing.

The conversation moves on to shopping and bras, but I'm back on the train to work reading the headlines on my phone. The dread returns, displacing the Xanax, threading my ribs and curling around my heart, a thick snake. I can't shake the fear that new predators will soon be at all of our throats, tearing at the soft flesh, their teeth carving fatal wounds.

I open my mouth to express my fear, to warn them, but Nicole stands up to clear the table for dessert. She takes our plates, bloodied with sauce, to the sink, then resets the table.

"Time for that beautiful cake," she says.

The cake sits in the middle of the table, so white it glows.

Nicole slides a knife into the center and cuts out a slice.

"What the fuck?" she says.

"What?" I say.

"I think . . . I think there's a cockroach inside the cake."

My stomach calcifies into rock.

"What the actual fuck?" I say.

She lifts the slice into the air and all of our eyes are on it: a shiny black bug buried in the sponge. The underbelly of the cockroach is thick with white sugar, its many legs suspended in sweetness.

I gag as my body seizes with panic and shame. My cheap cake has been found out, the faceless women in the puffy vests are judging me, I will never be invited back to this place, a place I'm not even sure I want to be. The shame burns away the Xanax and wine and I'm suddenly too sober to stand the humiliation. The pinprick of the void expands above my head and for a moment,

I wish it could devour something—the cake, the women, Nicole, anything.

But luck is on my side. Maria's head and shoulders slump and she lands facedown into her empty dessert plate, and Nicole screams that she knew we were high, shrieks like a crow flitting about the kitchen, the cake forgotten as the women gather around Maria, shaking her, trying to rouse her. I let them handle her this time. I've seen it all before.

Only later, after the shared ride home, our bodies collapsed in the back seat of a nondescript sedan, after slurring goodbye as Maria tumbles out of the car, after the driver continues on to my house, after I haul my body out of the back seat, after I fumble with the keys, after I find my way up the stairs, after I wash my face with cold water, after I strip off my clothes, after I climb into bed, the room spinning around me, only then does the full force of dread come crashing over me again, that same unshakable fear that something terrible is coming, and the black hole feeds off my terror, expanding, taking up the entire wall of my bedroom, growing so big that I lose myself in the deep darkness, the scent overpowering me, and as it rotates, I almost disappear, for a moment I am almost gone, as if it has already pulled me into the mysterious void, into the vast unknown.

museum

/ myü ˈzēəm/

noun

1. a building in which objects of historical,
   scientific, artistic, or cultural interest are stored
   and exhibited.

e.g., My father taught me to love museums. Museums were our
places, together.

Before I left for San Francisco, he took me to the Museum
of Natural History. After the train ride to New York City, after
we wove through the crowds of tourists in Times Square, after
a short cab ride, after we paid the admission, we stood before a
gigantic diorama. There were two jaguars on a wide-open plain
at sunset, the sky painted pastel with a glowing sun stuck setting
behind purple mountains. It was a permanent sunset, my father's
favorite time of day trapped, suspended in the air.

The jaguars were golden with black spots and thick muscular
bodies beneath the fur. One jaguar stared directly at us, motionless eyes gleaming above whiskers. The stillness of its face was
unnerving. The other jaguar faced the mountains and the sunset,
its mouth parted, teeth glinting. It looked as if it was ready to
hunt the future.

The black hole hung over the plains, small and quiet for

the day. My father slid his reading glasses onto his face to get a closer look.

"Says here, the jaguar's jaw is so powerful it can crush small skulls and even pierce the shell of a turtle." He shook his head. "Wowza."

"Crazy," I said.

He'd brought me to this museum because he'd been preoccupied with getting older. He didn't say it explicitly, but I could read between the lines.

"I used to go there as a kid," he'd said. "I'd like to see it one more time."

It was the phrase *one more time* that rang in my head. Every once in a while, he would slip up and say something that caught me off guard: *Last time, Getting on in life, When this is all over.* What hung in the air after these phrases was the implication of his death, as if he was warming me up for it. Each time, I'd say: *Knock it off, Don't be stupid, You've got a long time left.*

At the Museum of Natural History, we made our way past the gigantic bones suspended from the ceiling in the shape of a dinosaur. We walked beneath the belly of a big blue whale. We navigated fossils, then the Hall of Human Origins, where my father gazed upon skull after skull after skull.

Then we stood before Lucy, a skeleton from the early hominids.

Behind the glass, what they'd found of her was suspended against a black backdrop, a smattering of parts: small bones turned beige from dirt and time, her few found ribs rippling out like water around a stone.

I stared into her face, which was really no face at all. Her head was just a stretch of jaw, a bit of nose or cheek, and a small section of skull. I tried to imagine her whole, fleshed, alive. I came up empty.

"She's 3.4 million years old," my father said, pushing his reading glasses up his nose. "Un-fucking-believable."

I nodded. Sometimes, when he spoke, I didn't know what to say back. I just wanted to hear him talk.

"You know, I remember when they found her," he said. "I heard it on the radio. I was driving my car, and it came on the news. Then they played the Beatles song."

I pictured him younger, dark hair and thinner, the radio playing.

"You've been alive a long time, then," I said, teasing.

"Well, I remember I went home and told my parents," he said. "And they just nodded. But it mattered to me."

"Why?"

"Well, your grandparents were religious. When scientists discovered her, it was proof of evolution."

"A big moment," I said.

"Life is a series of big moments," he said. "Some days, of course, you're out there digging ditches. Some days, it's just a Tuesday, you know? But then there are the big moments. And you have to save them in your heart, crystallize them, and put them in a glass jar."

"Which moments have you kept?"

"Marrying your mother. You kids being born. My first car. Sailing the islands. Our vacations."

His voice trailed off. The hall was dark and empty except for the two of us, the exhibits glowing all around us like the hearts of distant galaxies. I wasn't sure what big moments I had. I didn't know what I was saving.

I felt myself on the edge of crying. I wanted to hold his hand or hug him. But I flattened the swell of the sea inside of me and knocked his shoulder instead.

"What about right now?" I asked. "Is this a big moment?"

"The biggest," he said.

I tried to crystallize the moment. I tried to put it in the glass jar inside of my heart.

The next morning, hungover, I take a car to the art museum. My head throbs, my stomach feels swollen, my blood moves through my body like sand.

At the museum, I drift through rooms of photography, the permanent collection, the modern paintings. I search for a piece of art that will wrap its hand around my throat and squeeze.

The main exhibition features the work of Vija Celmins. The walls are lined with her drawings, and her sculptures stand at the center of each room. In the first room, precise pencil drawings of the universe and stars and the waves of the sea. In the next room, giant gray paintings of objects lit with heat: space heaters and hot plates glowing electric orange. The paint is so vivid that the radiance of the canvas tricks me into feeling warmer, as if the painting will burn me if touched.

A piece in the final room of the exhibit makes my breath catch: a burning car is slashed in orange and red, a man emerging from the fire with flames on his back, the blaze a part of him. The same feeling I had on the sidewalk watching the man light up returns, the familiar adrenaline of horror, a sick déjà vu.

Then a family enters the room, a screaming child in tow, elbows bumping me, jostling to see the painting, pushing me out of the way. The moment is no longer mine.

———

After the museum, the black hole swells above me in my living room. The upcoming work week always makes me anxious, tension growing in my shoulders, my jaw, between my ears. This dread feeds the hungry spiral, which grows so large it takes up most of the ceiling.

The word *dread* evolved from the Old English *drædan*, meaning *to shrink from in apprehension or expectation; to fear very much.*

When the black hole gets this big, it's hard to pull away. It's hard not to look deep inside and lose myself in the abyss.

Other ways I attempt to stave off the black hole:

- Meditation

- Journaling

- Walking

- Making a list of nearby objects

I begin: blue velvet sofa, bookshelf, dead flowers, television, painting of the sea, trash can, unlit candle.

The black hole draws closer to me anyway, its metallic breath on the back of my neck. I attempt a meditation. On the floor of the living room, I close my eyes and picture a lush green forest. I walk slowly through a path, and all that fresh oxygen fills my lungs. I can hear a river in the distance. I follow its clear sound, a peace growing inside my chest, until I come upon a clearing lit by golden rays. But there in the clearing is the black hole, almost winking at me.

As usual, the calmness from the meditation doesn't last long. I can never hold my thoughts back, and the stress of the workweek flashes through my mind: more secret meetings, performance reviews, the CEO's demands, Sasha's needled face.

I open my eyes. The black hole has widened, matching the length of my body, a bad mirror, floating above me, stretching in tandem with my panic, blossoming in its power. The telltale hum grows louder, rushing over me, the song as cold and clear as a river.

A dozen candidates for the role in Pakistan appear on my screen in rapid succession. The video interviews are held during US working hours, which means the first begins at 1 a.m. local time for the candidates. They are bleary-eyed as if recently roused from deep sleep while dressed in their best business clothes. Some dial in from darkened rooms, their parents or partners sleeping one room over or on beds behind them, motionless lumps beneath comforters.

The first candidate is a YouTube star turned PR consultant with a focus on social media. Her résumé moves when I open it: a portfolio of the social media stories she's produced for major brands.

"I just, like, really believe in turning a brand into something accessible," she explains. "Like, right now? Your brand? It's okay. But it needs to go viral. You need a Snapchat."

The candidates soon blur together: some reveal themselves as less qualified than their résumés made them seem, some are out of college and desperate for work, others speak of working for a Silicon Valley–based company with stars in their eyes.

"It is the dream of me and my family to become part of the technology landscape," one candidate says. "Silicon Valley is the center of the world."

The interviews go on for hours, one after the other, until I'm no longer in my body, I'm a void. After the last call, I close my laptop and stare out the window at the bay. The men are washing themselves in the water again. Their number has doubled.

That afternoon, the CEO makes the weather change. He does this once a year, a display of man's power over nature.

The subject line of the email says: *Snow Dayyy!!!*

"Snow Dayyy!" a developer shouts before he runs away from his desk.

The email: *As per our annual tradition, please meet us in the parking lot for a snow day!*

We normally work until 6 p.m., but today everyone stops what they are doing. I've never seen them stop working before: they leave their screens, they come alive and excited, they become—for a moment—human.

I close my laptop and join the throng of Believers in their puffy vests and half-zips. We take the stairs and burst out of the building into the parking lot, the sun beating down on us.

It's my first time seeing this and it is magnificent. There, beneath the palm trees and the California sun, a gigantic hill of snow sits on the black asphalt. Beside it, a red machine churns out new snow, which floats down on all of us. I open my mouth and catch flakes on my tongue, the cold taste proving the scene isn't a hallucination.

The Believers waste no time. They snatch up black inner tubes and blue sledding disks from stacks beside the small mountain and start climbing. They sled down in reckless twos and threes, screaming the whole way, greeted with cheers when they come down to earth.

More Believers arrive by the minute, snapping pictures, posting them on social media accounts with the company hashtag. A cramp tears through my abdomen. I tell myself it's just my period coming on. Then I pray it's just my period coming on.

"You going to take a run down?" asks Jeremy, suddenly standing beside me.

"This is insane," I say. "How much does this cost? It's gotta be a fortune."

Jeremy shrugs. "I don't know. They do it every year. They can't stop now. It's tradition. Plus now with the press always covering it . . ."

A woman in a pink power suit stands in front of a local-news camera with a microphone in her hand as another pair of Believers speeds down the hill, landing in the giant pile of snow at the bottom. "It's that time of year again!" she says into the camera, her smile megawatt.

I haven't seen snow since my last holiday back east. A flood of homesickness hits me, a hollow feeling as everyone celebrates around me. Through the falling snow, I see the CEO standing next to Sasha, both smiling like benevolent gods. I wonder what it means to be happy. I wonder if they are.

"That's your blue RV over there, right?" I ask Jeremy. "I'm curious about living in one of those. I don't know how people do it."

His RV sits on the other side of the parking lot.

"Do you want to see it?" he asks. "Everyone does. I'm happy to show you."

A match ignites, a fuse burns down to a mass of black powder, ending in a burst of light. I want more of him, to see inside his mind. Isn't that what we all want? A way to peer inside the space of the other?

"Yes. I'd like that very much."

The tender paleness of the back of Jeremy's neck guides me across the parking lot. Small hairs curl over the collar of his T-shirt. Sometimes, all it takes to fall in love is one small detail: the back of a neck, the space between a thumb and a forefinger, a fleck of gray in green eyes, the wildness of someone's laughter.

No one notices us as we drift away from the snow and over to his gleaming RV. With each step we take, I'm more aware of his form: he moves with purpose but he's also loose, confident, calm.

"Now don't judge me. It's a little messy."

"That's what everyone says before they show someone else their clean house," I say.

He lets out a sharp laugh. "True. But it's . . . it's different with a smaller place."

"I won't judge you," I say, injecting reassurance into my voice. "I'm excited to see it."

Each of us has a dark room within our souls where we hide our truest selves, all the softest and weakest bits. Maybe his RV will be like that, I think: all of what keeps him alive in one place, squeezed together. He opens the narrow door and we climb inside.

"It's not much," he says, shrugging. He has to hunch as he

makes his way to a small bed with a blue-and-white comforter.

The RV is a tight fit for two people, but the interior is gorgeous and thoughtfully arranged: dark wood floors, hammered tin ceiling, and windows draped with white curtains. Modern wooden countertops and a small sink sit beneath slate blue cabinets, and a very small table features two seats.

"Would you like some green tea?" he asks, gesturing at an electric teapot.

"No, I'm okay."

"How about a seltzer?"

I nod, and he opens one of the cabinets to reveal a miniature refrigerator. He cracks open two cans of lime seltzer and hands one to me. A photograph of a very skinny woman in a bikini on the beach is taped to one of the cabinets. She is statuesque and tan, laughing into the camera with blindingly white teeth, the exact sort of woman who would be his girlfriend. Now that I've seen her, my heart pinches itself, extinguishing the small hot flame of my crush.

"She's beautiful."

"She?"

"Your RV. I can picture you putting everything together."

"It took a long time to outfit," he says. "But it's all mine now."

He pulls out his phone and presses a button. Music plays from somewhere within the RV, something slow and acoustic I can't place. But I nod as if I know the song well.

"Great song," he says.

"Reminds me of back east. I get homesick sometimes."

"I do, too," he says. "It's so weird out here. Like everyone is doing so much so fast that they aren't human anymore. It wasn't like this in the Midwest."

"Do you believe in what we're doing? Prometheus, I mean?"

"I've gotta do what's right for the company. Comes with being one of the first hires."

"How long have you been here?"

"Five years, which have gone by so fast. I'm not even sure what I've done with my life in that time other than work."

I run my hand over the cold, sweating can and take a sip.

"Do you like it here?" he asks.

"I don't think so. It's all too much all the time. Even today, even now."

"Now in here?"

"No, not in here. Out there."

I look into his eyes, which are softer and kinder than I remember. We are two planets passing each other in orbit.

The possibility: one of us could alter our trajectory and with it the whole path of our lives. Our lips could touch and perhaps we'd fall in love in a single second, get married, conceive at the perfect time, watch my belly swell with child, which would then emerge from me, slippery and without strain or effort, as if our son had always been of this world.

But the woman in the photograph is at the edge of my gaze. Her belly button winks at me.

The moment passes. The RV isn't the dark room of his soul. It's just a place to sleep, a place to live. A cramp passes through my abdomen and I wince.

"You okay?" he asks.

His eyes are so kind that the words rise up in my throat and I almost tell him: *I'm terrified, I might be pregnant, I'm floundering here, I'm so lonely.* But I don't know who I can trust.

"I'm just fine," I say with a weak smile.

"We should head back," he says. "They'll be looking for us."

We climb out of the RV and I trail him back to the mountain of snow. Endorphins flood my veins, as if I had been standing on the edge of a skyscraper, every cell of my body prepared to jump before I stepped back.

There are moments of beauty and light. It would be a lie to say it is all dread here. Even an oil spill has a rainbow sheen, an iridescent shimmer that trembles over its darkness. Life is this way, too: half suffering, half beauty.

Before it was applied to marble statues and women, the word *beauty* began as a word for objects, or for the light from God, or for a point in time, e.g., the moment a fruit was perfectly ripe. There are moments I am perfectly ripe, too, moments when I am the fruit bursting with the reddest of seeds.

The chef pulls up in front of my apartment in a restored dark red convertible. I put on my sunglasses and slide into the passenger seat. I tell myself not to think about my late period for the entire day and place the thought in a drawer in my mind.

"Where are we going?" I ask.

"Not telling," he says.

His hand is on my thigh as he guides us over the Golden Gate Bridge. We weave silently up the coast. The vibrant turquoise of the ocean never fails to steal my breath, and the black hole is a freckle on the face of the blue sky.

I can hardly let myself steal a glance at the chef, at the silhouette of his features against the sea. It's as if looking at him too closely might make him vanish. Happiness seems like a mirage, a trick of the light that will dissolve.

Finally, we pull into a rocky parking lot next to a wooden shack on the water.

"I wanted to surprise you," he says. "This is my favorite place."

"What is it?"

He pulls me close to him, and his mouth finds the pink shell of my ear.

"Oysters and champagne," he whispers, and a thrill runs up my spine.

We sit at a rickety wooden table on the water, the oysters spread before us in circles, plates upon plates of them, their gray mucus sparkling in the sun.

"I've never had oysters before," I say.

"Really? Well, I'll teach you all about them."

The texture of the oysters triggers a wave of nausea. I suppress a gag. I press my stomach with my fingers. Pregnant women should not eat raw shellfish. Pregnant women should not drink.

I take a gulp of champagne, and it bubbles down my throat.

He picks up a giant oyster. "This is the heart," he says, pointing at a spot of dark gray. I lean over and peer into the shell, at the heart of the oyster. "Oysters can change sex; this is their organ."

It pleases me: the idea of the oysters shifting, their mercurial nature a kind of freedom.

"What else do you know about oysters?" I ask.

"Oh, too much, really. They help control the tides because in large numbers they can hold back huge waves from shore. Their blood is colorless, which is why they look so bland."

"They look disgusting!"

"They live in cute little neighborhoods in the sea, clustered together."

"I love that. That's beautiful." I memorize the description, lay a bread crumb trail so I can return to the fact later. "The word *oyster* comes from the French for bone and shell."

His eyes light up over the table, two stars in daylight. "That's what I like about you. A strong mind."

"I know how a pearl is created. Bits of sand or dirt get inside the oyster. The pearl grows around the irritant as protection."

"Yes! But we're not eating that kind today. Anyway, you have to try one. Here."

He squirts a slice of lemon onto the gray sludge in the shell, then spoons red sauce on it. He lifts the shell to my mouth. The gesture is so romantic that I almost rear my head back. The scene feels too much like a movie, too much like a life that isn't mine. I fight to keep my head still, then part my lips. He tilts the shell and the oyster slides into my mouth. The flavor is a wave of brine and seafoam paired with the sensation of swallowing a second tongue.

He pulls the rough jut of the shell from my lips. I'm not sure if I like it, the oyster, but I know that later, in the evening, I want to trace his skin, I want his body close to mine. So I smile for him now.

"Incredible, right?" he says. "These are the best oysters in the state."

I nod and sip more champagne. A sweet drunkenness grows inside of me. He puts his hand on my thigh and I flush. Whenever he touches me, I feel as fluorescent as the lights in Las Vegas, as if my bones are glass tubes filled with neon, atoms exciting each other until they glow bright pink or violet.

For a moment, the thought of his girlfriend rises in my mind, a specter. I shake my head and push her ghost away. I let the sheer loveliness of the afternoon overwhelm me. I squeeze his hand and try to crystallize the moment in my heart.

Up above us, the sun blazes, that almost-perfect sphere, which will one day consume us, all of us, me, him, everything, engulfing the whole world in an endless white light before cutting to pure black, to absolute nothingness.

sex

/ˈseks/

noun

1. (chiefly with reference to people) sexual activity, including specifically sexual intercourse.

verb

1. determine the sex of.

e.g., The first time I had sex, I was on vacation in Las Vegas. It was also my first time on a plane. First, we were in the air, then we were on the ground, then we were out on the strip, me and my college friends, women I only see now through updates on social media, but back then, we were surrounded by fluorescence, our mouths open and laughing under the pink, blue, yellow, green, violet lights, our hands pulling down the silver levers of the slots, losing big, winning big, gin on our tongues, and I found a man, a tall one with brown hair and clear blue eyes like ice. I forget his name now, but he said, "I'm a military man, based in Alaska," and I liked that, the idea of Alaska, how far away it seemed, how it had forests and glaciers, how I had heard it was so cold in winter that your eyelashes froze. I even loved the shape of it, Alaska, and I loved the softness of the military man's voice, how gentle he sounded. I followed him upstairs to the blank clean slate of his hotel room and let him undress me and lay me down on the very white sheets, where my body tensed beneath his, and I felt a searing pain, a widening of self, a sensation in red I could never have imagined adequately beforehand, though I had tried, I had tried many times, but there I was, beneath him, his muscles pressed against me, and I gradually loosened like a baby tooth, then fell out. After, when he finished and was cleaning himself in the bathroom, I lay on the big white hotel bed and felt the new space, the new void that had been created inside of me, and finally I understood the nature of the black hole.

e.g., Later, when he was clean, he pulled me up from the bed. He smelled of water, of hotel shampoo, of mouthwash. Me, I was still covered in the scent of him, my mouth fuzzy from gin and his tongue. I was light-headed when I stood. I was a woman of experience now. I was a woman who could be anything. I was a woman who left three drops of blood on the white sheets.

He glanced down at the new constellation between us. See also: Orion's Belt, the Summer Triangle.

"That was your first time, huh?" he said.

I nodded.

"I wish you'd told me."

"Why?"

"I just . . . I should have known. Was it nice for you?"

I nodded again. Then my fake self rose up and took over.

"It was nice for me," I said politely. "Thank you very much."

Then he took my hand and we wandered through the hotel hallways, me still dazed, and we made our way down to the hotel buffet. It was half full of oddly paired couples, and there were silver trays of food that had been sitting out for hours: pale macaroni salad, baked beans, limp green lettuce. He steered me to the fried chicken, which sat under orange heat lamps.

"This is secretly the best fried chicken in Vegas," he whispered before filling a plate for us to split.

In a booth, we ate the fried chicken—it was delicious, he was right—and every now and then he'd place his hand on my thigh, leaving smudges of grease, and I could almost see the loops and whorls of his fingerprints in the glistening fat on my skin. I ate ravenously, suddenly starving, suddenly no longer caring what he thought of my appetite or the way my teeth tore into the meat.

"Had a fun time with you," he said with a little smirk, as if he was proud he had done something to me, proud to be the first man to alter me forever, the first man to put a new wound in me.

"You, too," I said. "Everything was lovely."

It was peeling out of the air between us, how we had been so intimate but knew nothing about each other.

"This chicken isn't so bad, either, you think?"

"It's very good. Thank you very much."

"You're a quiet girl, aren't you?"

"A little tired, is all," I said. "But tonight's been wonderful."

The black hole hung over the buffet, as if it were part of hotel security, another surveillance camera.

Later, we stepped out onto the glow and sparkle of the Strip. He pulled me into his arms and kissed me. Then we parted ways, him to wander back to Alaska, and me to find my friends, the grease on my lips and thighs shining beneath the lights, me with two fresh dents: one on my body, and one on my heart.

The next day, the relentless stream of candidates from Pakistan continues. Their hopeful faces flicker past me like a movie montage.

I keep an eye out for red flags: unexplained gaps in employment, half-hearted enthusiasm, lack of understanding about the tech landscape, failure to memorize the VOYAGER company mission. With every interview, I am also screening for a special resilience: Can this person survive Sasha?

After four hours, the last candidate of the day dials in. He sits in a brightly lit room and wears a blue button-down.

"Hello, Cassie! Wonderful to meet you. My name is Noor. I am excited to speak to you today about VOYAGER. I believe you are driving tech to the next level."

Throughout the interview, he's excited, knowledgeable, and hungry for the chance to work for us. Even better, he parrots our company mission like an echo of the CEO:

"VOYAGER connects everyone through shared use of global marketing data to drive ROI," Noor recites. "And I believe in that mission."

"So outside of work, what's important to you?" I ask. "I'd just love to know a little more about you."

"I live close to my parents," he says. "They have a farm. I go there all the time to help with the cows. I love that. It is important to me, you know, my family."

"I understand," I say, lying.

"That is why I was so excited to see an opportunity like this so close to home," he says. "But even if it wasn't, I would still want to work here. There is nothing I would not do for VOYAGER," he says.

I'm so impressed I pass him through to the panel interview with Sasha.

"We're cashless," the cashier says the next morning. He peeks up at me from beneath the brim of a black baseball cap with *Solidarity* stitched across the front in white.

"Cashless," I repeat.

"Just so you know. Some people try to pay with money, and it's, like, you know, get with the times."

I pull my card out to pay, and with this action, I realize I haven't carried cash in more than a year. Currency evolved along-side us: first the bartering of barley, dates, wool, the shaping of bronze rings. Then the minting of coins stamped with animals and dignified profiles, and then the printing of paper, each advancement a new signifier of value. Along with money came the concepts of gifts and debts, the ability to share wealth and also to owe payment, when men in Mesopotamia passed coins from palm to palm, the women looking on, unable to touch.

"Are you ready to pay or . . . ?" the cashier asks.

"Sure, sorry, sorry," I say.

"It's cool. People zone out in here all the time," he says, ges-turing around. "Real zombie hours."

No one reacts to his comment. The Believers are all around us, clicking at their phones. I imagine leaning across the counter and sliding my tongue into the cashier's mouth and not a single person looking up from their screens.

My eyes land on the one exception: a new mother in all black yoga clothes leaning over a black stroller with a baby inside. I try to calculate how many days or weeks late my period is. Time is so blurry I can't remember. I cycle through a list of comforting excuses:

- Stress

- Not eating enough

- Change in sleep schedule

- Thyroid issues

- Drugs

I'd slid the small bag of cocaine into my jacket pocket after doing my usual line before I left for work. I could feel it burning through the fabric of my coat, evidence that I was losing my ability to move forward without the powder.

"You forgot to put your card into the slot . . ." the cashier says, tilting his head at me.

I run my card through the reader. The transaction happens silently, the exchange invisible. The women of Mesopotamia return to me.

Suddenly, it comes back to me again, the relentless memory. I see the man on fire: his burning body, his mouth contorted into a silent scream, lifting a flaming hand, waving off help, a way of saying *No, no, I've chosen this.*

––––––––––

I find an empty seat on the bay side as the train lurches to the office. Through the window, the water reflects the dark gray of the clouds, doubling the silver of the prestorm sky. The scene is split in two by the long milky white shard of a great egret, which spreads its wings and takes flight.

I pull out my phone and read the top headline of the day:

CDC Warns New Virus Will Run Rampant in Coming Weeks

I picture the virus, invisible and insidious, entering the pink tissue of lungs and multiplying. I can almost hear the virus moving toward us, like the approaching hooves of angry horses, wild eyes glinting in the sunrise.

All of this information rushes in, all the terror of the new day. The world is distant and at the same time right on top of me, on top of us, its knife at our throats. We are everywhere all at once all of the time now. We are digital witnesses to each other's tragedies.

The black hole dilates in response to the news, as if we both know the virus is on the horizon, picking up velocity, aiming directly for us, the future not a bright light but a bullet.

At my desk, I forget which day of the week it is. The office is nearly empty, and I am grateful for the silence. I try to push thoughts of the virus from my mind. Exhausted, I begin my work: I click through emails, compile data points, then assemble a presentation.

"You're here early," a voice says, shattering the peace.

Corbett appears next to me, wearing a rare company fleece, testament to his five years of faithful service to our mission.

"Morning," I say.

"Morning! Thought I'd get a head start today, too! And I was thinking we could take a walk. What do you think?"

I look out at the bay, which is choppy at high tide beneath the dense gray clouds grown fat with future rain. A lone man is bathing in the water.

"Sure!" I say with false cheer. I have no choice and he knows it. "Let me just get my jacket!"

The air has a harsh chill. We begin our walk along the bay and pass the man bathing. A nausea rises. I can't tell if the sickness is from the cells likely multiplying inside of me, the sight of the man's bare chest in the cold water, or the anxiety of being asked to "take a walk."

Here's why: when someone in the Valley asks you to take a walk, it means you have fucked up. To be taken on a walk, especially with a supervisor or a CEO, is to be confronted with the harsh truth that you have produced subpar work. The benefit is that once they have delivered the blow, they can leave you outside to process your failures so you don't bring negative energy into the office environment.

As we walk, Corbett tents his small hands the way all men tent their hands in the Valley.

"Now, we need to discuss the errors on your new white paper. Are you open to receiving feedback at this time?"

"Errors? The team really seemed to love what I pulled together. The analytics look good, too. We saw a nice increase in downloads and lead generation."

"I owe it to you to give you more detailed feedback. Again, are you open to receiving feedback?"

He keeps his hands tented as we walk. How do men like this become themselves? Where do they acquire their power?

"Yes, I am open to receiving feedback."

"It seems like you don't understand the technical difference between iOS and Android. The technical section read as if it wasn't written by an engineer."

"I had the engineering team read and fact-check that section."

"I think it would have been better if you learned to code."

"Code?"

"Either way, you've been here less time than I have, so I thought perhaps some guidance was in order. Not guidance per se, but rather a bit of advice and change in placement."

"A change in placement?"

"Yes, moving forward, I should be the one to handle the technical writing. You clearly don't understand the back-end part of our technology, which means you don't understand the backbone of our company. You have so much on your plate anyway, and this comes easily to me."

"But I like working with the engineering team. I don't understand why this is happening. The results were great. And I'm pretty sure you're not my boss?"

"Well, I spoke with Sasha before I came to you, of course. She agrees with me," he said. "Sometimes we have to be flexible in order to do what's best for the company."

I picture it: him talking to Sasha about me, both of them shaking their heads over my performance again, disappointed, Sasha sending Corbett to me like a henchman to do her dirty work.

"What's best for the company . . ." I repeat, unsure what else to say.

"So, you understand, then?"

"I understand," my fake self says, since I cannot find the words or my mouth.

"Wonderful," he says. "Now, as a next step, we'd like you to take a coding boot camp. There's one that runs every weekend in the city. I've already got you signed up for the Sunday session next month."

He watches my face closely to see my reaction to the suggestion that I should lose one of my only days off from work. I hold my face very still. I won't give him the satisfaction.

"Thank you," I say.

He untents his fingers and slides them into the pockets of his fleece.

"I enjoy our talks, don't you? I always have."

Back at my desk, my fingers run wild over the keyboard. I message my friends and email my father about Corbett and our walk. I think of the long nights I worked on the project, of how well received the work had been, about the analytics proving I wasn't a failure. I think of how Corbett had done none of the work, how he wasn't even qualified to do what I did, and how I'd let him push me aside.

Still furious, I walk to the bathroom. In the beige stall, I pull the small bag of cocaine from my pocket. I measure a bump out onto the knuckle of my thumb and snort the powder.

For a moment, the drugs make me feel sharp and pristine.

But then a wave of nausea hits me, and a tide of bile rises in my throat. I fall to my knees and retch.

When it subsides, I wipe my mouth and rest my forehead against the toilet. I rest a hand on my swollen abdomen.

"Are you okay?" someone calls.

I sneak a look beneath the stall and don't recognize the electric purple shoes.

"Uh, what?"

"Are you okay? You sound really sick."

I reach deep, beyond the sickness, beyond the pregnancy, which now seems very real, and summon my fake self.

"Oh, I'm totally fine! Just this new supplement I'm taking didn't agree with me."

"It doesn't sound like that, it sounds really bad."

"Oh, I'm totally good! Don't worry about me!"

"If you say so . . ."

Whoever she is washes her hands and leaves. I retch again. When the heaving stops, I whisper to myself the list of reasons my period could be late like a mantra: *stress, not eating enough, change in sleep schedule, thyroid issues, drugs, drugs, drugs.*

The words don't comfort me anymore, but I keep repeating them, spiraling down into the anxiety of what I fear being true: *stress, not eating enough, change in sleep schedule, thyroid issues, drugs, drugs, drugs, stress, not eating enough, change in sleep schedule, thyroid issues, drugs, drugs, drugs.*

The black hole floats above the toilet, the only witness.

Notes & Research

- For the rest of his career, Hawking worked alongside his peers to disprove his own black hole information paradox. When he died, his colleagues continued the work.

- Their research was essentially an effort to maintain the laws of quantum mechanics and physics as we know them—and to prove information wasn't lost in a black hole forever.

- After forty-seven years of research, they had a breakthrough.

membrane

/ˈmemˌbrān/

noun

1. a thin sheet of tissue that forms a boundary separating two environments within a plant, animal, or fruit.

2. the pliable material that acts as a barrier between sections of a fruit, such as the white membrane that separates the groups of seeds inside a pomegranate.

Sasha's hair is freshly highlighted and her forehead is freshly frozen. She wears a new golden bracelet with the phrase *Lean In* hammered across the cuff, a VOYAGER hoodie, and designer yoga pants.

She's just flown back from giving a huge presentation on data and cellphones and engagement at a tech conference. She's great onstage, more electric than even the CEO. Something happens to her when she's in front of a crowd. Her bitchiness evaporates, revealing a powerhouse. No one can look away. Her presentations generate new pipelines in key markets for our sales team.

"Hey," she says.

"Hi," I say. "How was Berlin?"

"I was in Bangkok. And I got back last night. Not that you were paying attention. We're going to have a very big year there."

"Really?"

"Yes, e-commerce is exploding there," she says. "And we have the best user data right now. I got our foot in the door with a few white whales."

I nod, not caring.

"I met with the Pakistan candidate," she says. "Noor."

"Oh! How did it go?"

"Surprisingly well. I didn't think you'd find anyone worthwhile. But he's hungry, and he seems ready to fight for his place here."

"I'm glad you liked him," I say slowly.

"And he already lives near the Lahore office, so I think this will work out."

"I made sure I was only interviewing candidates who live near the office," I say.

"Anyway, do you have some time to take a walk?"

"Of course! Sounds great!" I say, my heart sinking into my stomach under the heavy weight of familiar foreboding. "Let me get my jacket!"

Along the path, the fat heads of the purple flowers flop in the hard wind as the storm gathers strength. There are no men in the bay. Only a few birds bob on the surface of the water.

"I know we haven't caught up in a while," Sasha says. "I've been so busy."

"Me too! So busy. But that's what I love about this job!"

"I wanted to check in about how you've been feeling lately."

Paranoia flashes through my veins. Could someone have already told her I was puking in the bathroom?

"I'm fine."

"Well, you know, you could tell me if you weren't," she says.

My face flushes, I can feel it. Can she smell the vomit on my breath?

"I would tell you," I say. "I trust you."

I prepare another series of lies: *I bet it was something I ate, I don't even want a child, I'm dedicated to the company.*

"Well, anyway, I also wanted to talk to you about something that isn't work related. It's about eggs," she says. "My eggs."

"Eggs?"

I imagine a chicken egg, floating next to her head. I see a cross section, and I label its parts: *eggshell, albumen, vitellus, membrane*. The Egyptians incubated eggs inside underground caves, delicate eggshells beneath tons of sand and hard black rock.

"Well, I am trying to harvest my eggs."

"Oh, I didn't . . . I didn't know that."

"Yes, I want children one day. And since I'm single . . ."

"Right, of course."

"But it's hard! And expensive!" she says. "My eggs keep failing. They failed again this morning. The doctor just called."

She reaches down and lifts her shirt.

"This is where I do the injections. Every day. It hurts like hell. And still, no eggs."

Her protruding belly is covered in bruises and angry needle marks. The thought of her sliding those needles deep into her own flesh brings on a flood of nausea. I wince but cover it up with a nod.

"I'm sorry," I say. "That must be so hard."

"Do you know anything about egg harvesting?" she asks.

"No, I don't. Sorry."

"I was hoping you would. I was hoping another woman would know."

Her eyes look damp. For a moment, she's not Sasha from the office. For a moment, she's merely a woman suffering. And for a moment, I wish I could pull out what might be growing inside of me and give it to her. The black hole hovers in front of my belly.

"I'm happy to listen if you need to talk."

Her face contorts and morphs back into the Sasha I've always known. "I don't need to talk. I need my fucking eggs to come out. My friend has been working with a shaman and says she's getting more viable eggs," she says. She stares out over the bay. "It's a shit ton of money, but maybe I should try the shaman?"

"That seems like it could work," I say. I try to make my voice sound encouraging to hide the fact that it does not seem like it will work.

"I'd love to figure it out before Burning Man this summer," she says. "If I can get my eggs harvested before Burning Man, I'll be in great shape. We're taking a private helicopter out there."

The world divides again: Sasha in the helicopter with or without a batch of viable eggs, and me at my desk, praying I'm not pregnant.

"Anyway," she says. "There was something else, too."

A new dread surfaces. She fluffs her hair.

"We need to talk about your performance," she says. "Corbett came to me and told me he doesn't believe your work is up to par, either. It isn't just me who thinks you need to step it up."

"Step it up how, exactly?" I ask. "I've been working like crazy, and if there's anything specific I can improve on, I want to do it."

"Corbett and I both agree that you need to learn how to code and dedicate yourself to truly understanding our technology," she says. "You've been here for a year now. We expect more, because plenty of others would be grateful for the opportunity we've given you."

Step it up. The phrase hangs there, vague and menacing. I don't know what more they want from me. I don't know what more I could possibly give. But what I know: in the Valley, there are thousands of new graduates who would jump at the chance to do my job for less money. If I miss a single beat, someone else will be standing at my desk. And apparently, beats have already been missed even if I am not sure which ones.

"Understood," I say. "I'll step it up."

She heads back into the office. I stand outside in the cold, imagining myself working even faster, faster than the speed of light, working so hard I become even more of a blur, not sleeping, not eating, woman as machine. I picture Sasha's insides, the pink of her womb, the eggs in her ovaries shriveling, already rotten.

I want to die at every biweekly All Hands meeting, and today is no different.

Rows of blue company-branded chairs are set up in front of a massive white screen. This is one of the only days bad food is allowed in the office. Today, there are gourmet churros.

"Can you believe they got churros?" a girl in a black beanie says to me. Her mouth is full of carbs, sugar on her lips, her eyes shining. She looks almost high, a kind of ecstasy normally reserved for drugs. "These have been all over Instagram and it's impossible to get them. We are *so* lucky."

"We are *so* freaking lucky!" I chime back at her.

I turn away from her and find a seat in the third row. Visibility is crucial. I spot the side of Jeremy's face in the front row.

After the early start and the walks and the vomiting, I feel tired and filthy. My face is greasy, and the smell of sweat wafts up from my jean jacket. Anxiety thrums through me as I try to ward off the thought that I'm pregnant.

It might not be true, it might not be true, it might not be true, I chant to myself to keep calm. *Stress, not eating enough, change in sleep schedule, thyroid issues, drugs, drugs, drugs.*

The CEO is at the front of the room with the rest of the founders. I shoot him a smile. He doesn't acknowledge me, but

I can sense he sees me. I look attentive and alert so he will see I want to be here, that I am ready to step it up.

"All right, let's get started," the CEO says, flashing his teeth above his expensive half-zip with the VOYAGER logo. Only the most elite employees get VOYAGER half-zips. "We've had a busy quarter and I'm excited about the energy of this company."

"Yeah!" a Believer shouts from the back. A smattering of laughs and claps break out.

The CEO smiles.

"Now, I've said this before, but I'll repeat it: we are on a very special journey together at VOYAGER."

He clicks, and a slide appears behind him: a VOYAGER-branded cartoon rocket ship being launched into outer space.

"I was talking to the rest of the C-level team about this the other day and I wanted to share it with you. We are on a rocket ship together. And this rocket ship is headed to the moon. The moon is us going public. Which we will, if you all keep up your hard work and dedication to our mission."

All the Believers applaud and whoop. The CEO takes a sip of water from a luxury water bottle, which also sports the company logo.

"Moving on. Today, we're going to kick things off with anniversaries," he says, clicking to a slide that says *Anniversaries!!!!!!!* above another rocket ship.

I fight to suppress a wince. The next two hours stretch out before me, a wasteland. We must endure certain things to prove our devotion. The stock options dangle over our heads, almost within reach.

I worked as a fry girl as a teenager. I stood under the red glow of a heat lamp before a metal tray that always seemed to be spilling over with french fries. I used a silver scoop to gather the hot, oily fries and slide them into red-and-white bags. At the end of each shift, my hair and uniform stunk of french fries and old grease. I can still feel the heat, smell the stench, taste the salty slick of my fingers. Now, here I am. Look at me. I have made it all this way for this.

"We're going to celebrate three employees today," the CEO says. "Sasha, why don't you come up and introduce the first one?"

Sasha steps up to the front of the room. I imagine the unharvested eggs in her ovaries, weak and thin, pumped full of hormones to no avail.

"Today I'm happy to celebrate the anniversary of someone I never thought would have lasted this long," Sasha says with a sharp laugh. "Things haven't always been easy. But today, we are celebrating *one year!*"

There is a hesitant smattering of applause. It is a milestone to last at the company for 365 days, to suffer the lunacy, the unrealistic expectations, the insane hours.

"She's worked really hard to learn our company and our values and continues to try to overcome the learning curve. Anyway, today we'd like to congratulate her. *Come on up, Cassie!*"

To my horror, the CEO clicks to the next slide to reveal a gigantic image of my face, set inside a yellow star, next to the words *One Year*.

All of the eyes are on me. I feel exposed, as if they can see right through me, as if I am nude, as if they are judging every feature of my body. Another round of applause roars, but quickly dies down as I make my way up to the front. Jeremy's eyes are on me. His gaze burns through me.

Sasha shakes my hand and the CEO hands me a backpack with the company logo as someone snaps a picture.

"Thank you," I say.

My head spins at Sasha's pivot from cruelty to praise.

Then I remember that a portion of my stock has vested as a reward for my year of service. Suddenly I can push through my exhaustion and perform the scene. "I am so pumped to work at such an incredible place. Here's to the rocket ship we're on! Here's to many more incredible years at VOYAGER for all of us! We are *going to the moon!*"

"*Yes!*" the CEO says, clapping. "That's the energy! That's the *energy*!"

The room erupts with more applause at the CEO's manic excitement. As I make my way back to my seat, a few Believers pat me on the shoulder or shoot finger guns, nodding their approval. I've passed another unspoken test. I sit back down.

My stomach feels hard as a rock. I want to walk into the bay. I want to let the water swallow me.

An hour later, I run into Sasha in the kitchen.

"Sasha," I say. "I had a quick question about my stock."

"What about it?"

"Well, since I'm vested, it's mine now, right?"

"Yours?" she asks.

"Yeah, like it's my stock now? I own some of the company?"

"That's not how it works," she says.

"What do you mean?"

"Well, it was clarified in your job offer. After the first year, you have the option of purchasing the stock at thirty dollars a share."

"That's not how the initial offer was worded."

"I think you misunderstood the legal language."

"But thirty dollars a share is really high, right? It would cost me"—I do the math in my head—"eighty thousand dollars to buy all of my stock?"

"Do I look like an accountant? That's the deal. You're employee 201, and that's how things work when you get into the game that late. Besides, when we go public, it'll be worth it."

"Worth it," I repeat, dazed at everything I've lost in this one conversation.

"Anyway, you need to close out that Pakistan hire by the end of the month, so get moving. This is on you. You told me you were a leader when I hired you. So be a leader."

She walks off, leaving me alone in the kitchen. Fury burns my face, my pulse thrums. The black hole seethes alongside me, widening like a screaming mouth.

inner horizon

/ˈinər həˈrīzən/

noun
1. The inner horizon lies entirely within the outer horizon of a black hole.
2. The inner horizon is the boundary of the region from which light cannot escape.

e.g., Also known as the Cauchy horizon, the inner horizon is where the black hole's gravity grows strong enough to keep light from leaving, but not strong enough to drag it all the way into the center.

It is known as a chaotic place: matter falling into the black hole collides with matter being flung outward by the centrifugal force caused by the black hole's rotation.

Past the threshold of the inner horizon, cause no longer necessarily precedes effect, the past no longer necessarily determines the future, and time travel may be possible.

e.g., After graduation, I wore cardigan sets and pleated slacks and sensible shoes. From nine to five, I went to an office and sat in a gray cubicle at a cheap desk and worked. I made to-do lists, I attended meetings, I made phone calls, I made spreadsheets, I made jokes calibrated to a shared office culture, I attended the mandatory functions. The black hole was always with me.

e.g., Once you get one job, then you get another job, and another job after that, and on and on. The years accumulate. Nothing about me had changed except the scale of my life: I got a new job or a promotion, I moved into a bigger apartment, I wore new clothes, I went to dinner at fancy places where the food was served on small plates. My emotions went blank, and I moved through each day as if in a meaningless dream.

Through it all, the idea of the inner horizon tormented me: If you could reach that place, could you reverse time and change your life? Would it only take you into another dimension, into a different future in a new world? Or would the force of it shred you to oblivion?

Believers surround me on the packed train home, our bodies pressed together. Sometimes their hands graze my lower back or the fat of my upper arm. I can smell all of their homes, buried deep in the fabric of their clothes, and if it is not their homes, it is their breath, their weak all-natural mouthwash or lunch caught between their teeth.

Towns whip by as we make our way to the city. Exhausted from anger, I slide in my earbuds. I try to transport myself somewhere else, anywhere but here: a street in France or a beach in Colombia or a castle in Lisbon, or the green clearing from my meditations, but I can't sustain a single illusion. The pressure of the workday hangs on me, a dead albatross pulling at my neck, the stench of it choking me.

A few feet away, I see the girl from sales again. Her face is melted into her phone, her fingers moving rapidly over the screen, texting, smiling and glowing brighter than the screen, as if she might be in love.

There is a dangerous liminal hour after I get home from work, before I go to meet Maria and Nicole. I sit on the sofa in silence and try to relax. But the black hole spirals open before me.

My life flashes through my mind: Noor's kind face, my

nonexistent stock, Sasha's needle-marked stomach, Corbett's milky skin and doughy paunch, the CEO's endless energy, the hometown power plants belching out cloud after cloud, my father on his knees, in the grocery store, stocking shampoo.

A terrible panic rises in my chest and before I realize it's happening, I'm seized by anxiety: my heart thrashes in my chest, I can't breathe, I break out in a fever, fear overtaking my ability to grasp reality, I'm sure I'm dying or going crazy, my body shakes, I'm sure I will never come back from this, this is eternity, this is forever, this is what it feels like to go insane, this is what it feels like to die.

The wave passes. I'm drenched in sweat. I look around and name five things in the room: trash can, couch, table, bookshelf, candle.

My heartbeat slows. But then the black hole draws nearer and hovers in front of my stomach, as if it is the father of whatever might be growing inside. I swear I can feel the glob of cells dividing in my uterus, expanding, turning toward the black hole, speaking its language, singing its own song back into the void.

A new terror flashes through my mind: a child born to me, a little girl with a small black hole of her own trailing her into this awful world, two cords tethering her back to me: one red, one black.

Outside, I pass a newly boarded-up Italian restaurant, a failed laundromat, a shuttered bookstore. Next to them, a new storefront window frames a giant robotic arm that is serving lattes to a small smiling crowd. Five men in black high-performance jackets pass me on one-wheel hoverboards.

Maria and Nicole wait for me in front of the old movie theater. Despite the dramatics, I'm glad to see them. I don't want to be alone. A historic marquee glows above our heads. Inside is all old opulence: high ceilings, golden lamps dotting the red velvet walls.

We stop at the concession stand, where Maria orders two double gin and tonics and carries them to our seats with a smirk on her face. Nicole and I trail her with our popcorn and diet sodas. I sit between them.

"I've had a long day," Maria says, tugging one of her curls.

I almost let out a bitter laugh, but I don't want to have to explain myself.

"It's always a long day for that one," Nicole mutters.

"What happened?" I ask.

"You know I can't talk about it," Maria says.

"Don't baby her," Nicole says. "She's a grown-up."

"You're such a tease," I say.

"At least I'm not being sued within an inch of my life," Maria says.

She slips a white pill into her mouth.

"Don't tell Mom over there," she says. "You know, the pills don't always work. Sometimes it's like they do the opposite of calming me down."

"I don't know why you started hanging out with her," Nicole says in my other ear. "She's always fucked up."

But Maria makes sense to me: she is smart and sharp and fast and sad. Most days, it feels like we are the only two people tracking what's happening in San Francisco, the only ones who understand exactly how bad things have become.

The previews begin. On screen, a man kisses a woman. Their

faces are gigantic, their mouths pink and pressed together, the camera so close that their lips look like creatures from the deep sea. I fall asleep before the opening credits.

When the lights come on, I wake up. Maria is slumped in her seat. I nudge her shoulder.

"Get up, sunshine," I whisper.

"Oh, real surprising," Nicole says.

Maria opens her eyes with effort.

"What's up? What the fuck did she say?" she says. "We going?"

"Movie is over, Ms. Pills," Nicole says. "Time to go home."

Maria wobbles as she stands. I grab her elbow to steady her. We make our way into the lobby, which is ringed by vintage arcade games.

"I want to play Donkey Kong," Maria says, stabbing a limp finger in the general direction of the game.

"Come on," I say. "Time for bed."

"Why," she says, slurring. "Because I'm *fucked up*?"

A few people startle at her outburst and turn to stare. Nicole's eyes widen like she is going to snap. Then she does.

"Yes, because you're all fucked up," Nicole says. "You're always fucked up. All you do is get fucked up!"

The eyes on us multiply. Shame floods my body, an ancient shame, a shame I know well.

"I am not fucked up! This city is fucked up! Maybe you're fucked up!!" Maria shouts. "That's what this city does to people. You just refuse to see it!"

They keep screaming at each other. Their voices echo through the theater. Screaming isn't new to me. It reminds me of my mother. But the whole city is like this, everyone here is so on edge that the yelling is constant.

I step through the glass doors, into the night. I'm too exhausted to stay and watch.

"And where are you going?" Nicole says behind me, an accusation.

I don't give her the satisfaction of turning around. I pass beneath the glowing marquee, then take a left toward my apartment. I walk past noisy bars crammed with techies and locals, past food carts and a knockoff shoe store. Drunk men stand in front of a convenience store and whistle as I pass. The sidewalks are covered in piss and shit.

A brief fantasy carries me away: driving to the sea with the chef again, gesturing at the waves as I list all the blues for him: cerulean, turquoise, azure, holding his face, my thumb on his bottom lip, handing him my dripping heart with our bare feet in the sand. My mind can make love out of anything, even the smallest of shards.

I snap back to reality when I reach my apartment building. The man who sleeps beneath my window is on his knees screaming into the sky as I unlock the front door. I can feel it coming.

"You're a *fucking bitch*," he says. "You really are! I see you every day! I know, trust me, I know what you are!"

I hang my head and step inside. A white envelope is taped to the front door of my apartment, my name scrawled across the front. Ripping it off the door, I step into the quiet of my living room.

Inside, a letter from my landlord outlines the following: my lease is coming up for renewal, and based on current economic conditions, my rent will increase nine hundred dollars.

The amount is so staggering that I lose my breath. I sit down on my couch with the letter in my hand like a snake, which I drop once the message finally lands in my brain. I almost expect it to slither away across the floor.

I crawl into bed and try to sleep, but the city is relentless. The figure $900 wraps its invisible hand around my throat and squeezes. The man under my window cries out again.

"I'm bleeding," he howls.

There is a chorus of breaking glass and the sounds of what reminds me of a wounded animal.

"I hate it here," he says, then screams: *I hate everyone, fuck you, fuckers, fucking fuckers, fuck this planet, this planet fucks me, I've been fucked by the planet, I hate it here, fuck you, fucking fuckers.*

The city wears away at all of us, wrenching open mouths full of a rage that explodes out of us, turns us into self-immolators or sacrifices to commuter trains or people who relentlessly scream our pain into the night.

motivation

/ˌmōtəˈvāsh(ə)n/

noun
1. the reason or reasons one has for acting or behaving in a particular way.
2. the general desire or willingness of someone to do something.

e.g., Why would I stay here? Why do we do anything in our lives? Is it always driven by motivation or desire? What might begin with a passionate choice can turn into paralysis or lethargy once that decision has been realized and the newness wears off. A single choice made with the best intentions can become a terrible life. Imagine biting into a seemingly ripe fruit, only to have your mouth filled with rot.

e.g., On my first day at my job, I was covered in the shine of the new. I thought I was starting over, fresh. Maybe moving across the country had cleaved all the wrong parts from me, slicing the rot from the fruit, leaving behind the clean flesh. In those early days in the Valley, the black hole was minuscule, a blip I could almost blink away. I was high on this lightness, briefly, as if my old body had died, and my new body was taking shape. I was dazzled by the palm trees, the dispensaries, the sun against the sea, the freshness of the vegetables. I laughed at jokes from the grocery store cashier, I bought a pair of earrings in a boutique, I drank expensive green juice. I felt like someone else.

e.g., I chose the path and then I walked it.

"I love it here," I chirped to my father on the phone.

"I knew it," he said. "I am so goddamn proud of you. You took a chance, you did it. Look at that."

A wild, bright pride filled my heart. I wasn't a doctor or a lawyer, but I was still someone to be proud of, a child grown into a capable adult with a fancy job title and a new life in California, a daughter who had gone west in search of gold—and found it.

e.g., But slowly, the tide receded and the trash beneath the water was revealed: the money was not as much as it had seemed after taxes and rent. The work schedule wore down my enthusiasm. My energy dropped as I slept less to work more. On weekends, I slept late to make up for the long hours at the office. My boss began commenting on my weight, my hair, my clothing.

"Why aren't you wearing your company gear?" she would ask. "We give it to everyone for a reason. It's part of our culture."

Impossible tasks landed on my desk: work all weekend, attend every event, write a three-hundred-page report on the state of the industry in three days. My life in San Francisco started as a trickling stream of clear, pristine water. Within weeks, it was a swollen, polluted river, and it was no longer mine. I was choking beneath the surface, a hand outstretched, mouth full of filth, treading water, fighting for breath.

By the end of my first month, I was another faceless woman on the train, falling into the bland rhythm of nameless days.

Soon I was a volcano.

There are many ways to tell if a volcano is likely to erupt.

Over and over, the same train, the same scenery, the same towns whipping past through the windows.

A volcano erupts in several stages. Movement begins in the earth's crust, creating an increase in tremors and earthquakes.

Over and over, the sun rising or setting, the coffee between my knees as I tapped at a glass screen, the late nights, the eye of the company on me.

Animals near the volcano become agitated. Gases are released from seams that run along the sides of the volcano.

Over and over, the dire headlines, the limp salads, the walks along the bay, the insane expectations.

Lava dome buildup, lava dome collapse, magmatic explosions, more dome growth interspersed with dome failures.

How many identical days can a person live before she explodes?

Finally, ash, lava, and pyroclastic eruptions.

board the train and then the headlines yell the world back at me again.

First Virus Death Reported in the US

Experts Warn of Intense Wildfire Season on the Horizon

Rent Protest Planned in SF

I click on the last headline. My jaw tenses as the page loads. The article details: rapid rent increases, developers' plans to tear down affordable housing in favor of luxury apartments, soaring rates of unhoused people, the cost of being here and the cost of staying here, developers driving out longtime tenants, luxury apartments going up on block after block, the city's plan to build plywood sheds to house the unhoused.

Outside the train window, the streets are empty of bodies. All the bodies are on the train, going to work. So am I. I can feel the building of my body burning. I want to take my burning body to the street. I want to scream.

I drink a cold brew, then go to my desk, already wired. For once, Sasha looks up at me right away.

"Morning," she says, flashing me a smile.

"Morning!" I say.

"I wanted to circle back with you about Noor's offer. I haven't seen anything come through. What's the status?"

"I was checking his references. They've been great so far, but I'm waiting on the last one," I say.

"You always have an excuse, don't you?"

"It's not an excuse—it's how we hire people here," I say weakly. "But also, I've been really busy working on that big presentation for you and the CEO. The one about ROI? You asked for it a few days ago?"

I've prepared a deck, a series of slides that offer concepts and calculations and ways to increase revenue and take down the competition. The thought of standing up in front of them makes me nauseated. A small ache radiates from my lower back. I feel a headache coming on. I want to go back to sleep, to put my body into a bed and never rise again.

"Oh, I won't see it. I'm leaving early to go see the shaman in Mexico about my eggs."

"What?"

"My helicopter leaves at two."

"But I thought you said I had to present to you today."

"Just wanted to keep you on your toes," Sasha says with a smile. "Besides, you are senior level. You should be able to present to the CEO without me in the room by now."

My pulse quickens. The world sharpens. I think I smell gardenias. I open my laptop and pull up the presentation. I click through each slide, refining language, tweaking numbers, increasing the size of the graphics. All around me, Believers work in silence.

———

I head to the big meeting room where the CEO is waiting. I take a seat across from him.

"Looking forward to this," he says, grinning.

And then I do what the company asks of me. I shove everything down—the chef, the possible pregnancy, the rent increases, the imminent wildfires, the virus—past my white ribs and red heart, into my belly. The black hole, now expanding, hums loudly next to the whiteboard.

You wake up one day and realize what you've become, what you allow, and you have to stare down into the pit at yourself, at your own choices, at the ways in which you have been cunning and stupid and false and wretched to keep up with the world around you.

How does anyone bear themselves? How can anyone stare into the darkest corners of humanity and return to the office, enter the meeting room, and deliver the presentation? How do we all just keep working?

The CEO nods at me. My fake self opens her mouth and begins.

On the days when the sadness grows unbearable, I take myself to the sea.

After the presentation, I sneak out of the office early since Sasha isn't around. I'm sure Corbett will rat me out, but I don't care. I take the train home and get changed. Then I tap my phone screen. Two minutes later a car pulls up in front of my apartment building. I slide into the back seat, my empty skull reverberating with the echo of work.

"How's your day?" the driver asks.

"It's okay, how about yours?"

"Busy! Strangely busy."

"That's good!"

"Where you going?"

"I want to see the beach. Work was crazy."

"Sorry to hear that."

"It's okay, just how it is."

"You smell good. What's that perfume you're wearing?"

I allow his question to hang in the air for a beat too long.

"Just something I found at the store."

"It smells nice, real nice."

"Thank you."

"You, uh, you got a boyfriend? He's letting you go to the beach alone?"

"I do, but he's working tonight."

I can feel his eyes on me through the rearview mirror. The car grows smaller then, suddenly suffocating.

The same epiphany I had in the office returns: I have no control over the world around me, or the people around me, or how they regard me, or how they speak to me. A fury beats in my heart, which is where fury comes from, where it lives, in its red home.

The car pulls up beside the beach.

"Enjoy the beach," the driver says. "Your boyfriend is a lucky man . . ."

I could spin into a storm, a woman turned hurricane, all wild winds and violent rain. But I am too sad to muster the strength, too tired, too lost, too faded, too limp.

The late afternoon sun is slung low in the sky. I slide off my shoes and walk on the cold sand. The black hole follows alongside me above the shore.

The sea here is sharp and salty, almost mean. It is a sea too cold to swim in, which means it is mostly for decoration or a nice place to cry. The sky is beginning to pink. The occasional black rock juts out of the water and birds perch on their highest points. The occasional bonfire burns, outlining the gradually darkening silhouettes. The occasional pair of lovers embraces in the surf. The occasional dog runs and frolics. The occasional surfer in a bodysuit paddles out to meet the frigid waves.

As I make my way down the beach, the melancholy expands inside of me, matching the size of my second shadow. The word *loneliness* evolved from the word *oneliness*, which did not connote lack. It meant a time to commune with God. But what if you don't believe in God? What happens then when you're alone?

I look around at the people, at the sky turning peach at the bottom of the horizon.

A group of Believers enjoys a picnic. They wear their puffy vests and drink their IPAs. I count them: nine Believers, nine vests, nine pale hands holding pale ales. They are laughing, nine open mouths with white teeth in perfect rows.

In another world, I can see my fake self at their picnic, laughing and drinking. Is that what part of me wants? Or is it only loneliness and fear making me wish I could become a Believer?

My sorrow is so great that it becomes a knife between my ribs. The cold sea runs over my bare feet. The horizon is a flatlining heartbeat. The black hole floats over the waves, a negative sun against the still, pastel sky.

I am suspended in the nothingness of the middle of life. There is no one to turn to and say: *Isn't this just beautiful?* as the sunset screams its final brilliant colors.

I see the back of her head first: dark brown hair streaked with gray. She is sitting at a table outside a restaurant, across from the three identical girls from the dinner party, all in matching vests.

I'm on my way to the rent protest at city hall with Maria. It is Saturday, late afternoon. The sky is a perfect blue, no clouds. Maria holds a sign that says Rent Freeze Now. Her rent increase is $750. Groups of protesters make their way in the same direction, a purposeful river.

I consider not acknowledging her at all. But at exactly the wrong moment, her head turns, and she catches sight of us.

"*Girls!*" Nicole says. "Oh my god, *girls*! Come here! Get your asses over here!"

We both sigh as we make our way toward her.

"What are you two *up* to?" Nicole asks.

"We're on our way to the protest," Maria says, tugging a curl.

"What are we protesting today?" one of the girls in the puffy vests asks.

They are Believers at brunch. On the table: bottles of champagne and orange juice and four half-full glasses. In the center, a shared plate piled high with French toast topped with whipped cream.

Maria shakes her head and looks away.

"There are rent increases happening all over the city," I say. "Including in my building. And Maria's. We're in the middle of a housing crisis, it's all over the news. How could you miss it?"

"Oh yeah, that," another vested girl says from the hole in her beige face.

"Yes, that," I say. I wonder who pays her rent.

"I guess since I have rent control, I haven't been keeping up with all of that, either," Nicole says. "Why don't you two put those signs down and have a few mimosas?"

"I don't think so," Maria says.

"We've had, like, really long weeks at work," the third vested girl says. "Like, we're fried."

"Plus, protests don't do anything. Like, have you thought about running for city council or something?" Nicole asks.

I shoot a look at Maria, who is shooting the same look at me.

"You know, I'm still thinking about that freaky cake," one of the girls says with a smirk.

"You're a fucking bitch," Maria says.

"Wow, Maria," Nicole says. "Why don't you, like, calm down."

"Tense much?" the girl says.

I give myself over to the fantasy: I am punching her in the face, luxuriating in the satisfaction of my fist against her flesh, the way her nose pops beneath the pressure, how the blood streams like garnet from her face, rich and sparkling, a sign that I have changed her.

I grab Maria's arm.

"We need to get going," I say. "Enjoy your brunch."

"Have a great protest, ladies!" a girl says.

They return their attention to their food, lifting forkfuls of sweet bread and whipped cream to their lips. Their world stays the same. It is as if we were never there at all. Our two realities coexist without overlapping.

At city hall, people gather in small groups. Soon we are one mass beneath the gold-gilded architecture.

The signs surround us: *Rent Hikes Are Unjust. Make SF Affordable Again. ALAB.*

Maria and I chant along: "Ban rent hikes, ban rent hikes."

The police surround us. At first, they're almost pleasant. But as the hours pass, the crowd grows. Nothing violent happens, but the size of the protest makes it seem unrulier than before.

Suddenly, a new group of police steps forward. For some reason, they are wearing black Kevlar vests, black helmets with black shields covering their eyes, black batons in their hands.

"Why are you in riot gear?" a protestor shouts.

The cops stand silently. They don't flinch or turn their heads.

"You don't need riot gear for this," another protestor calls.

"Don't come out here dressed like that!" another one says.

A man with a bullhorn leads us in a chant: "No riot gear, no riot gear."

We stomp our feet in rhythm.

The energy of the crowd is so strong it crackles. A policeman in full gear steps forward with a bullhorn of his own.

"This is the city police department. This gathering has grown too large and you do not have a permit. You must disperse. This is your warning. You have two minutes to leave the area."

I glance at Maria.

"Fuck them," she says. Her usual paranoia is gone.

"We're not going anywhere," she says, louder.

"*Hell no, we won't go*," she shouts, and the crowd joins her, protester by protester, until everyone is bellowing the same phrase.

"We have warned you," the policeman says through his bull-horn. "We will now be taking action."

We chant and chant and chant. For a glittering instant, the possibility presents itself: what we can do if we move as one. A new future appears before us, incandescent, a world of peace and beauty, a world of affordable cities.

And then the illusion is shattered.

A white fog of tear gas billows up over the crowd. Screams rise. Gunshots give way to the sound of rubber bullets hitting flesh. Cries of fear and pain tear through the night as the crowd disperses.

Maria and I turn and run, dropping our signs, our feet pound-ing the pavement, my heart in my throat, screams in my ears, chemicals in my mouth.

We dart down an alley and come to a stop, panting. Maria shakes her head, hands on her knees. Sirens wail, and protestors are dragging along those who have been tear-gassed or shot.

"Fuck those motherfuckers," she says.

She presses a white pill into my palm and then pops one into her own mouth. I exile the word *pregnant* from my mind as I swallow.

———

Monday, on the train again with coffee, the sun hiding behind gray clouds, the bay silver beneath the gloom. I scroll through the headlines.

Second Virus Death in the US

Rent Protests at City Hall Turn Violent

Wildfire Breaks Out

Homeless Man Found Dead in the Mission

I check my work email and my heart sinks. An event invitation appears with the subject line: *Emergency Mandatory All-Hands Meeting.*

I sigh and let my head fall against the dirty window. I close my eyes. I try to forget where I'm going.

There are plates of exquisite fruit again: dragon fruit, passion fruit, figs, the bellies of the pomegranates split open. I gaze into the red mass of seeds. No one touches the offerings.

A quiet panic rises up from the room. Emergency meetings are reliably a sign of something terrible: an acquisition, layoffs, a loss of stock.

The blue branded chairs are arranged in neat lines. I sit in the third row.

The CEO stands before us, a grim look on his face. Through

the windows behind him, the bay is at high tide beneath the thick gray sky, which is gathering the energy to release another storm.

"Everyone take a seat," he says. "Let's get started. I'd like to make this quick."

Bodies shuffle at the sound of his voice. Sasha sits in the front row next to Jeremy. She is back from Mexico with thin silver feathers woven into her hair. Once we are settled, the CEO takes a sip from his water bottle, then clears his throat.

"Today I wanted to take a moment to address two things happening in the news."

We all shift in our seats.

"First, I wanted to talk about the virus. We have formed a small team to keep a close eye on the situation. This team has developed a contingency plan that we will follow in the event of a local outbreak. The plan includes mask requirements and safety measures. As you know, we do not believe in working from home. So do whatever it takes not to get sick. That is your responsibility to this company."

We all nod.

"Now, to get out ahead of this, we've got hand sanitizer for everyone. Please make use of it."

He holds up a small bottle of hand sanitizer with the VOYAGER logo splashed across the front.

"Any questions?"

We shake our heads. A blue plastic bin full of the bottles circulates among us.

"Good. Okay, next we need to talk about something sensitive."

We shift in our seats again.

"The latest tech industry diversity report is coming out tomorrow," the CEO says. "I need to say right now that I do not agree with our ranking in the report."

We squint at the CEO, wondering what will come next, wondering who wrote his script.

"I won't get into the details. But I want to state firmly that this company stands for equality, and we are already making incredible strides in our inclusion and diversity initiative."

We look around the room. There are only three employees of color. We nod in their direction in sympathy and in solidarity.

"And this is my promise to you," the CEO says. "We will work to make our company more inclusive. Thank you."

We clap, as we are supposed to. Perhaps we're applauding the words he said, a gesture at leadership, at being a human. Perhaps we're applauding inclusion and diversity. We're not sure what we're applauding, but we applaud. Then we get back to work.

Noor's face fills my laptop screen. He looks bright and excited despite the late hour in Pakistan.

"Good morning to you, Cassie," he says.

"Good evening to you, Noor," I say.

"It is nice to see you again. I had a wonderful time at the panel interview. VOYAGER has a fantastic marketing team."

"Yes, that's what I wanted to discuss with you! You did an excellent job."

"Oh, really? That is lovely to hear. Thank you, thank you. I especially loved speaking with Corbett and Sasha."

When he says Sasha's name, a reverence comes over him, as if he is speaking of a saint.

"I finished checking your references," I say. "And I'm excited to be able to extend an official offer to you. We think you would be an excellent fit for our team, and we'd love to have you work at VOYAGER as our PR point person."

His face goes electric with joy.

"*Oh, Cassie!* Cassie, Cassie, this is the best news I could hope for! I loved everyone on the team. This has been my only dream."

"You did an excellent job throughout the interview process, Noor. We're really thrilled to have you join us. And we're offering you a starting salary of twenty-five thousand dollars with a signing bonus of three thousand dollars. We've also included a generous stock package."

His excitement reaches a new level.

"Oh my god, Cassie. Oh my god. My family will be so proud. I promise to work so hard for VOYAGER. I will work day and night, at any hour. You have changed my life. I am so excited!"

"We're so excited, too, Noor," I say. "I'll have the written offer sent over ASAP. It will need to go through a few approvals on our side first."

"You will not regret this," Noor says. "I will repay you for this opportunity through hard work. I am so excited!"

The screen goes black and the fake smile fades from my face. I know what I have done.

It is another meeting about the destruction. The CEO and Jeremy both sip beige liquids. Electric from too much caffeine, I've leapt the hurdle of my own physical exhaustion and become my other self: sharp, focused, ready to make pointed assertions.

"Okay, let's talk Prometheus," the CEO says. "We've already

implemented Cassie's first round of ideas, and we're seeing a big uptick in traction. But I'm ready to explore some darker options."

We all nod. The CEO looks at Sasha.

"We're not slashing any car tires, but I want to talk about real ways to destroy Nomad."

Sasha glares across the table at the CEO. The tension between them is stronger than before. I wonder what battles they are fighting in the other meetings, in the bigger meetings, the ones where the C-levels debate above our heads.

"We could sabotage their upcoming conference," Sasha suggests, running her fingers over a delicate chain around her neck that spells out *Spiritual Gangster*. "Plant haters in the audience."

"Haters?" Jeremy says slowly, as if the word is foreign.

"Well, people who would ask hard, targeted questions about how they use data. It would ruin their event and reduce trust in their brand."

"Maybe," the CEO says. "But come on, we have to do way better than that. A few planted questions aren't going to get the job done."

Imagine a clear stream, I think. Imagine a mountaintop, nimbus clouds, volcanoes erupting, galaxies colliding and combining their stars above our heads. Imagine your blood cells churning through your body, through the miles and miles of veins and arteries and capillaries. Imagine nuclear bombs, ancient whale sounds, tundra filled with flowers in bloom in the snow, jaguars, millions of children being born at this very moment, millions of women splitting in half at the same time to make way for the screaming, bloody future.

"We just need to take their servers down," I say. "The outage will shake up their customers. We'd need to take them down for a day, max. It would make the news and definitely scare the market about Nomad's ability to keep data secure."

The idea spills from my mouth before I even realize it, my fake self delivering what the CEO wants. He stares directly at me, a new sparkle in his eye. A woman's value increases when a man looks at her as if she is an equal. It's a rare occurrence, like standing beneath a clearly visible solar eclipse.

"It's perfect," the CEO says. "Genius. It's the first step to shake the public's confidence in their product."

Sasha and Jeremy are so disgusted or so jealous they cannot meet my eyes.

"Who would do it?" the CEO asks.

"We could hire someone," Jeremy suggests. "It needs to be an outside job. Then we can post it on the hacker message boards and the press will pick it up."

He's right: the tech press here is always hungry for blood, and the stories break within minutes if they can take down a hot company.

"An outside job," Sasha repeats to prove she is still in the room.

"Yes, hire it out. But only one more person can be involved. The circle stays small," the CEO says. "Good job today, Cassie."

Jeremy shoots a small smile across the table at me. Sasha pulls out her phone and begins tapping at the screen in defiance.

"Jeremy, I want you to execute," the CEO says. "This is a great next step, but I don't want to stop with taking a few servers down. We need to keep inflicting damage."

"I know a guy who works quickly," Jeremy says. "He's the best in the business, but he isn't cheap. We won't do anything too crazy yet—just a data breach, but we won't take any information."

"You know the money isn't an issue," the CEO says. "You have a blank check as far as I'm concerned. But let's keep the ball rolling beyond this breach, too. We'll start meeting here on Saturday mornings."

Jeremy nods. My chest crumbles like ancient ruins at the thought of losing my precious, golden Saturdays. Chunks of marble fall into a crashing sea.

"Can't wait," I say.

"Excellent," the CEO says. "Cassie, you're dismissed. We'll see you back here on Saturday."

Friday night again: we are on the couch, my legs draped across the chef's lap, my head on his shoulder. He has one hand between my legs, up my dress, resting there, making a heat build inside me. We watch a documentary about cuttlefish. On-screen, the cuttlefish shifts hues, fluttering beneath the surface of the sea.

"You've been so quiet this week," he says.

The cuttlefish have elastic pigment sacs called chromatophores that allow them to change colors for the purpose of eluding predators.

"Lots of work to do," I say. "I have to go into the office tomorrow."

I don't tell him the truth: about Noor, about the deceit, about sucking another person into the dysfunction of VOYAGER, about the destruction meetings, about the way I fear my mind is unraveling.

Changing the iridescence and pigment of its skin allows the cuttlefish to mimic nearby colors and textures, making for effective camouflage.

He squeezes my thigh.

While the cuttlefish does not see in color, it does register polarized light. This helps the cuttlefish determine how to mirror its surroundings.

"I hear you. There's this big dinner on Tuesday night and I gotta forage local herbs and source truffles."

Much like an octopus, the cuttlefish can release sepia clouds of ink to confuse predators as they escape to safety. Long ago, cuttlefish ink was used for drawing and writing.

"Are you going to make the black hole for dessert?" I ask, running a finger behind his ear.

The average cuttlefish only lives for two years.

"You and your black holes," he says, teasing, his eyes on mine, his hand moving farther up my dress.

We kiss, and my mind calms. I don't think about work or destruction or the CEO or Sasha's eggs or the needles sliding into her skin or Noor. I don't think of the chef's girlfriend or whether I can love him or really have him or the nausea or the looming fear that the clump of cells is still multiplying inside my womb.

Instead, I think of: our bodies, my dress over my head, his shirt open, all of it as natural as the cuttlefish flashing wildly, all bright and electric, vivid and iridescent, in the seconds before it dies.

The next morning: when I open my eyes, my head is against the chef's chest, my hand in the patch of dark hair. He has never stayed in the morning. It's been an invisible boundary in our relationship, as if the risk of that intimacy is too great, as if we'd come too close to breaking the one rule of his open relationship.

"Morning," he says. "Coffee? I can make some for us."

Us. I nod. The sun makes my room a brilliant, soft white. Nude, I curl into the sheets as he steps into the kitchen, shivering at the thought that he will crawl back into bed with me, that I will feel more of his body. I stretch, pleased, peaceful.

But it could be a fantasy, a mirage. If I blink it might shatter, like a rock through a mirror.

"You have to go to work soon, right?" he asks from the kitchen.

"In a little bit," I say. I run a hand through my hair, my fingers catching in knots. My breath stinks of wine, and a dull headache blooms behind my eyes. The pain feels nice, though, the poking of small knives reminding me I'm alive.

"Well, I was hoping we could spend a little time together first," he says, returning to the bedroom.

He hands me a fresh cup of coffee, then slides into bed, our bodies reuniting. His skin is warm and familiar. Soon, the fingers of his free hand run up my stomach to cup my breast, tracing my nipple until it hardens. The stirring begins, like it always does.

He takes the mug from my hand and puts it beside his on the nightstand. Then he takes both of my breasts in his hands, putting his mouth on them, then he is inside of me again, in the light of morning, and for the first time, our eyes are open, we are staring into each other.

A new feeling catches in my throat, as if my heart is trying to escape from my mouth. My eyes fill. For this one gorgeous morning, there is only us, no work or girlfriend or sadness, and he is mine and we are full of pleasure and each other. It is as close as I have ever come to love.

I do a line in the coffee shop bathroom before I get on the train. The powder cools the heat in my veins.

Time speeds, the hours blur, so do the weeks. I forget it's

Saturday until I'm on the train and realize there are no Believers. Instead, there are women in orange fluorescent vests with San Francisco Airport stitched on the back. Instead, there are women in black clogs wearing waitress aprons beneath their jackets. Instead, there are women carrying babies who occasionally scream, their newly red gums inflamed from teething.

When I check the news, our secret project has made headlines.

Nomad Servers Down:
Customers Lose Money During Outage

The article details how Nomad's customers have been unable to run their marketing campaigns for a full day because the servers are down. The result: $1.3 million lost in revenue so far, that number climbing higher every minute.

A flash of nervousness runs through me and my palms begin to sweat, as if everyone on the train can tell who I am and what I've been involved in. To distract myself, I click through a few more news sites before an alert lights up my phone. It is another breaking tech headline:

VOYAGER Ranked Last in Latest Tech Diversity Report

More stress floods my veins and I tuck my phone away.

Then I turn the morning with the chef over in my mind like a piece of hard candy on a tongue: our naked bodies in bed, the dawn light, our eyes open and searching, that rare new bliss opening a possibility of a relationship between us. The black hole is the size of my belly, hovering inches from it. I try to forget the headlines. I try to forget the black hole. I try to forget my swollen stomach. I try to forget my own life.

———

In the office kitchen, a quiet rage overtakes me that I'm at work on a Saturday. As it builds and combines with my hangover, I'm afraid it will take over and I'll do what I truly want: smash the coffee mugs and avocados, set fire to the ergonomic chairs, bash in the sleek screens of every computer monitor, black glass shards flying everywhere.

Instead, I pour myself some cold brew.

In the big conference room, Sasha, Jeremy, and the CEO are already brainstorming.

"About time you got here," Sasha says. "We've been waiting for an hour."

"Didn't you say to be here by eleven?"

"That meant ten, and you know it," she says. She looks angry, but her forehead is too frozen for her to glare at me properly.

"Sorry," I say.

I imagine: a tropical climate, a distant island, the deep blue sea, the cratered surface of the moon, the rings of Jupiter.

"Well, now that you're here, we need your help," Jeremy says.

I sit down next to him, grateful for the cover he's offering. He smells of verbena and sweat. Despite myself, I lean closer to him.

"What's going on?" I ask.

"Our plan has gone exceedingly well," the CEO says. "Yesterday we poached one of their biggest clients thanks to the service outage. But we cannot allow ourselves to grow complacent. I want us to brainstorm our next steps."

I imagine: a lush verdant jungle untouched by human greed,

a waterfall spilling over black rocks, a bioluminescent bay glowing blue in the night.

"I think now that we've taken their servers down, it's time to show their data is vulnerable," I say. "It's time to expose real information."

I cannot believe what my fake self has said, but she's already said it.

The CEO regards me as if I am Corbett or an oracle.

"Yes," he whispers, almost tenderly. "Yes."

"A data breach like that can ruin a company," Jeremy says softly. "No one will want to be associated with them."

Whenever a data breach happens, the headlines use words like *exposed* and *vulnerable*. I imagine millions of people stripped nude, their bare bodies shivering in the harsh blue air of the Internet.

My face flushes. I look away.

"Our guy can do that," Jeremy says slowly, as if he doesn't want to. "But it will cost more than last time."

"Make damn sure none of this gets traced back to us," the CEO says. "Get it done. I don't want the details. Pay in crypto again."

"How can I help?" I ask.

"Work with Jeremy to figure out what data to expose," the CEO says. "We need to do something powerful, but not insanely destructive. Sasha and I will be working on another plan that doesn't involve you two."

They stand and gather their things.

"We'll be at my desk," the CEO says. "Let's regroup in an hour. I'll expect there to have been progress."

"Oh, and Cassie?" Sasha says. "You need to compose that offer letter for Noor and get it to HR. You made the verbal offer, so get the paperwork done. I shouldn't have to follow up with you on everything like this."

I nod and sink back in my chair. The ruined day stretches out ahead of me.

I am not entirely sure what we are meant to do. My brain is fuzzy. Jeremy moves closer. Can he smell the sex on me? A cramp grips my abdomen, but I push the pain down.

"Let's do this thing," Jeremy says.

"Remind me, what exactly is the plan?"

"We need to determine where to focus the data breach," he says. "It will make the customer information vulnerable—we're opening a wound, for lack of a better term, and then stepping back. The question is: What type of wound do we want to open?"

I imagine a cut oozing data and information, the blood digital and blue.

"I see," I say. "So are we shooting them in the leg or in the heart?"

"Exactly. Emails and passwords?" Jeremy runs a hand through his hair.

"That would shake confidence, but I'm not sure it would get more customers to ditch Nomad for us."

We both fall silent.

"Since the emails and passwords won't do enough damage, we both know what's next," I say. "He won't want to stop there. He's too determined to take them down."

"I didn't think we'd stoop so low," he says. "Is this how you really are? You're ruthless."

"You're ruthless, too," I say. "I'm not sitting in this room alone."

"It's not like I started out that way. It's what happens when people come here."

"It's like being carried away on a tide."

We look into each other's eyes for a few seconds too long. In that moment, I believe we will both take a stand. We will say *no*. In the space between us, a million flowers blossom in the air, invisible and fragrant. A million possibilities open their soft petals like parting lips. A million possible futures bloom.

He sits back in his chair.

"Okay, that's our game plan," he says. "Banking information."

Everything that began to bloom suddenly wilts.

Sasha and the CEO return to the conference room. The CEO's eyes gleam, as if his internal mechanisms are electrified. His eyes tend to shine when he is close to brilliance. However he and Sasha spent their hour, they must have done something even more unethical than us.

"What did you come up with?"

Jeremy nods in my direction.

"We suggest exposing the banking information of their users," I say. "Since they pride themselves on top-notch security measures, this is an escalation that will cost them customers and keep their name in the headlines."

"We'll have our hacker get to work," Jeremy says.

For some reason, I think of my father's smile: his eyes like the clear sea, surrounded by sandy wrinkled skin, his nose bulbous and wide like mine, his mouth open in laughter, slapping his leg, his joy shaking the room. I think of our emptying town collapsing around him, and of our house falling apart, all he's worked for his whole life rotted by the slow, persistent rust of time.

"There's no looking backward, honey," my father said once. "Closure is bullshit. There's nothing in the rearview mirror. There's only the future."

The future is as cold and alien as the terrain of a newly discovered planet. Isn't that the beauty of the future? If you push forward, if you aren't too afraid, if you step into your space suit and enter the darkness, you will discover new and terrible worlds.

"We'll destroy them," I say.

"Get your guy on it," the CEO says. "But not a single fingerprint left behind, do I make myself clear?"

He looks at us with the severity of a king planning an invasion. I see him: the CEO in a robe of red, an entire fleet at his command, the towers of his castle visible behind his golden crown.

"Good job today," the CEO says. "And don't forget, I'll see you tonight."

I'd forgotten: there is a party at our top investor's house. Another mandatory event. My night to myself vanishes before my eyes and I swallow a sob of exhaustion.

"We'll be there," Jeremy says.

The white tiger uncrosses its paws and lets out a yawn. Its mouth widens to show teeth that hang like off-white stalactites over a pink tongue, yet another cave. The black hole, small as a pomegranate, hangs in the air.

"He's one of the rarest tigers in the world," Jeremy says from behind me.

He takes a sip of his vodka soda with lime. I hold a glass of red wine. My period is now more than two weeks late.

In the late afternoon sun, we stand on the lawn in front of the investor's looming mansion. His land spreads out before us, offering up tennis courts, two pools, and a giant sundial at its center. Gigantic floodlights hang above our heads, ready to blaze when the sun sets.

Every year, the investor invites his most promising companies to a party featuring exotic animals. As it turns out, every year, our company is invited.

Towering metal cages line the lush green lawn. Each cage holds an animal: a zebra, two bobcats, an old lion, a baby giraffe. There are other animals, too, ones we can touch: marmots, bald eagles, a small fox with wise golden eyes. There's even an elaborate temporary pool where two sad otters swim endless laps.

"I've never seen a tiger up close before," I say. "Let alone a white one."

I trace the pattern of its fur with my eyes, the white coat striped with winding black marks. The tiger regards me with lidded hazel eyes. Its massive clawed paws rest on the floor of its cage. Seeing the tiger should feel magical, as if the mystery of nature is being revealed to me. Instead, it feels pathetic. The animal is sedated, weakened almost to the point of sleep.

"I don't know. I've seen this tiger, like, five years in a row," Jeremy says. "I'm over it."

Across the lawn, Sasha wears a leather glove and holds a pure white owl. Just beyond her, an albino peacock opens its plumage and becomes a living snowflake. And beyond the rare peacock, the CEO stands with the investor beside a caged black jaguar.

"We should go say hello," Jeremy says. "We've already waited too long. I can't keep avoiding meeting this guy."

"Why don't you want to meet him?"

"Who cares about investors? They're all the same. The work is what matters. The company is what matters. But the CEO will be pissed if I don't go over there. This is the guy who backed Prometheus. Come with me."

We make our way across the lawn. The red wine sloshes inside my bloated stomach.

We nod at Sasha as we pass. She now has an old bald eagle perched on her arm. The animals get rarer and sadder as the party progresses.

"There you are," the CEO says as we approach.

The greeting is for Jeremy and not for me. But I nod and the CEO nods back.

"This is our primary investor," the CEO says. "I've been waiting years to get you two in front of the other. But Jeremy is too humble to take any credit for our success."

The investor does not look rich, but that's how they prefer to present themselves: they hide their wealth behind casual clothing and sneakers. They blend in with us. The investor has brown hair and blue eyes, the nose and chin of a different Greek god.

"Heard great things about you," the investor says. "You've been doing a bang-up job on Prometheus."

Jeremy nods, assuming correctly the investor couldn't be talking about me. In the cage, the jaguar stretches her body. Her muscles flex beneath fur so dark it reminds me of the center of the black hole that floats beside her.

"Anything for this company," Jeremy says.

"That's why I love him," the CEO says. "This *energy*. That's why I'm in this business. People with *this* energy."

We all nod in agreement.

"How did the latest project turn out, by the way?" the investor asks.

"Prometheus has been a massive success," the CEO says. "And all thanks to Jeremy."

With that, it's clear I will not be introduced. The investor will never know who I am. I'm invisible, woman as a ghost. I stay quiet. It's what they want.

The sun is setting in the pastel sky over the rich man's perfect lawn. The lithe jaguar paces in her cage. I stare into her yellow eyes. She isn't sedated. She is ready to pounce. Only the metal bars keep her sharp white teeth from our soft, bare necks.

The next morning, I wake filled with dread. I could carry on without knowing, but time keeps passing and soon it might be too late. The black hole hangs above me, close and menacing. The force of the abyss is so strong it almost keeps me pinned in bed, but I force myself to stand up.

I apply the basic makeup required to look human, brush my teeth, pull on a long black dress, and do a line. Outside, my street is overrun with mothers and strollers. The faces of the children are impossible to look away from: their cheeks fat from milk, their mouths stained green or brown from food, their eyes bright and innocent from knowing nothing of the world's horrors.

I trace my usual path to the grocery outlet. I turn left onto a quiet street where a woman is squatting in the middle of the side-walk. She wears a red sweatshirt, and her jeans and underwear are around her ankles. I don't register what I'm seeing until I'm staring: she is defecating on the sidewalk, in the light of day, beneath the fluttering fronds of a palm tree. The smell of it reaches my nose.

I step back, averting my eyes.

"Bitch, what are you looking at?" she says.

"Sorry, sorry, sorry, sorry," I chant like a madwoman. "I'm so sorry, I didn't mean to—"

"Keep your eyes in your fucking head! Shove those apologies up your ass, too!"

I walk back the way I came to find another route, face red as if I've been smacked.

In the grocery outlet, everything is all wrong. The beauty aisle is suddenly garish, a grotesque array of cheap items: off-brand razors in an awful shade of electric pink, expired mascaras in neon-green tubes, bright yellow bottles of old deluxe bubble bath, fading purple bottles of discontinued shampoo, hair dye in colors no one wants.

Women push by me with their carts as I stand there, pretending to be hypnotized and lost in deliberation: *Can I use it? Do I want it? Will making this purchase fill the hole in my heart?*

But really, I am waiting for the women to leave. I don't want anyone to see what I'm buying. As they mill farther down the aisle, I edge closer to what I'm looking for: feminine products. Unfamiliar brands of tampons and pads line the shelves, alongside douches and feminine washes.

My eyes land on the bottom shelf: the pregnancy tests. A new earthquake of anxiety rattles me as I kneel. The black hole floats down, hovering between me and the shelf.

The box says Equate in blue script. A white pregnancy test

is circled in hot pink on the front. The benefits are listed in light pink script: *Easy to read line results. Over 99% accuracy. Test five days sooner. Early detection of the pregnancy hormone.* The pink circle is feminine, joyous, hopeful. The pink circle says *I want a child, We've been waiting, All of my dreams are coming true.* I wish there was another brand of test, one in a plain dark box, one that knows I'm terrified.

The black hole moves nearer to the test. I reach around it to snatch the box off the shelf and stuff it into my basket.

Reality sinks in then: I'm going to know soon.

I make my way to the meat section, where the butchered bloody meat rests on soft beds of white Styrofoam beneath the glassy shrink-wrapped surface. I place a nearly expired slab of red steak in my basket next to the test.

In the produce section, I discover something surprising next to the aging bananas and the almost overripe apples: a single pomegranate.

I pick up the pomegranate, feel its weight, then drop it into my basket. I wander to the checkout aisle, a zombie beneath the fluorescent lights.

In my bathroom, I pull the horrible box from my canvas shopping bag. The same sensation I experienced in my last presentation to the CEO returns: my fake self takes over and it's as if I've left my body, which continues without me.

My fake self tugs the white stick from the plastic packaging, moves to the toilet, hikes up her dress, and slides her underwear down to her ankles. She positions herself over the bowl, sliding the stick between her legs, splashing a stream of urine over the plastic. When her bladder is empty, she slides her underwear back up and lets her dress drop over her hips.

She places the stick on the sink. The stick has two small windows. A blue line runs through the first window. If the second line appears, it means pregnancy.

My mind is floating, safe in a kind and soft space made of sweet white light. From up here, it doesn't matter whether I am pregnant or not. There is only the light of eternity. Here in the light, nothing can touch me.

Until the second line appears, ripping me from the warm light and back into my body.

The second line means nothing, really. It is pointless, it is only a symbol, a signifier. But the implication is massive, gravitational. The line is like the gamma ray burst I've seen in photos: a brilliant explosion in blue that stretches across the sky like the horizon of a new, terrible world.

I expect something violent to happen inside of me, to shake and tremble and quiver, either with fear or with joy. No feeling comes.

I want to cry or throw up, but neither happens. The sun shines through the window. Outside, the world goes about its business. From above the sofa, the black hole watches me.

I throw the stick into the trash and step out of the bathroom. I lay out two lines on the counter and snort them with a deliberate precision.

Notes & Research

- In a new paper, astronomers hypothesize that wormholes may actually exist in the center of black holes. Although research is ongoing, this new discovery undoes decades of calculations that pointed to anything entering a black hole being destroyed.

- The existence of wormholes has been debated. Einstein included wormholes in his theories about space and time, but we've never proven they exist. However, just like black holes, wormholes are considered a mathematical probability.

- Based on the new hypothesis, objects that enter a black hole may ultimately enter a wormhole—and be able to travel through space and time.

- It seems there are now two possible outcomes if you enter a black hole: you may be ripped to shreds, or there is a slim chance you will cross into another space and time, another dimension.

  - **Option One:** My body stretched, spaghettified, torn to pieces by the sheer force of the black hole.

  - **Option Two:** I survive, and I find myself in another dimension, another timeline, another life entirely.

seed

/'sēd/

noun

1. the fertilized ripened ovules of plants, normally capable of germination to produce a new plant.

2. the edible seeds of a pomegranate are also known as arils.

Denial makes me pretend it is still a normal Sunday. I find myself outside on the sidewalk, waiting for a car to take me to the art museum. I try to focus, but my vision blurs.

The cocaine buzzes through me, but I'm not numb enough. My problem is too big. It is the size of a child. I weep behind my sunglasses. The truth of it stirs up my insides, a tornado tearing through my ribs.

There should be some disruption, a rip in the fabric of space and time. But the world spins on, indifferent to the change in me.

The car pulls up and I get in.

"How's your day going?" the driver asks.

I want to scream: *I'm dying inside, I'm pregnant, I hate it here, I'm nothing, I'm not what I thought I was going to be, I want to die, I do, I want to die, what am I going to do now? I'm going to ruin my life, I am a mistake, my life is wrapping its hands around my throat, I'm—*

"I'm good," I say. "How are you?"

"You know how it is. Sundays are busy! Everyone wants to go everywhere—the park, the ocean, the museum."

His joy is clear and kind, which only makes my sadness larger in relief. I gather my strength to answer him, to play my part in this scene.

"The weekends are always like this here," I say. "So much fun."

"You like art?" he asks. His hazel eyes glint in the rearview mirror.

A sob attempts to escape, but I fight it down.

"I love art," I say, but the words come out strangled.

"You okay?" he asks.

I nod and look out my window, still crying quietly.

"I'm fine," I say.

"You sure?" he asks. "You don't seem so fine. A pretty girl like you shouldn't be crying, not on a weekend."

"I'll be okay," I say. "Just got a lot going on."

"Things could always be worse, right? There are children starving! And you're here, in this car, going to the museum."

He reminds me of my mother. A twinge of longing and fear twists through me. My mother would be disappointed with the mess I've made. My mother would be stinging.

I nod and continue weeping.

"Nothing can be all that bad," I lie. "I'm in the car and I'm going to the museum."

"Exactly," he says. "Choose happiness! Happiness is a choice we make every day!"

In the rearview mirror, his eyes light up with a big smile. Another sob tries to crawl up my throat, as if it has claws. I stuff it down, down into my belly, where I imagine the child inside of me must be sobbing, too.

art

/ˈärt/

noun
1. the expression or application of human creative skill and imagination, typically in a visual form such as painting or sculpture, producing works to be appreciated primarily for their beauty or emotional power.

e.g., The art museums have always calmed me the most. At the museum in Philadelphia, I once wandered into an unlit room. The black hole almost seemed to evaporate in that darkness, but it was just a few shades too dark to vanish completely.

Against the wall stood an old barn door. I shrugged in the dark, unsure what the point of the work was. But as I turned to leave, a bright light sparkled through a hole in the barn door. I moved closer to the peephole, bent down to peer in.

Inside was an elaborate installation. Beneath a fake blue sky: a landscape with a small river running along some barren brush, a nude woman holding a flickering lantern, her legs splayed open, the most private part of her exposed, on display.

Her body was so pale and marbled with veins that she could have been alive or dead, but she was so realistic I swore she was breathing. I brought my eye closer to the hole in the wood to be sure, thinking maybe she had died right before I found her. My heart lurched at the brutal honesty of the piece, of seeing her body like that, vulnerable and abandoned.

Anything can be a mirror, and my face stared back at me from her body. She was my double. A surge of tenderness washed over me. I stayed with her for a while, the way you might sit beside a dying bird on the ground, waiting for that final heave of the chest, that final breath.

The black hole floated through the door and into the installation, then widened over the body of my twin, inking out the false sky. Looking back, that moment might have been a warning.

In the museum, I go straight to the main attraction. The featured exhibit is from an artist I've never heard of: Alina Szapocznikow. Dozens of eerie, vibrant sculptures of the human body dot the giant white room.

In the first piece, *Small Dessert I*, a woman's mouth and chin, composed of skinlike resin, rest on a yellow cloth in a dish of sparkling lavender glass, as if her lips are being served for high tea. Where is the rest of her? Somewhere, a mouthless woman must walk among us.

There are sculptures of breasts and nipples displayed on glass cake stands, illuminated lips atop the stretched necks of lamps. In the corner, a sculpted body features glowing red breasts and a mass of blue mouths where the head should be. I stare at her, waiting, as if one of us might eventually come to life.

A dark form catches my eye. In the center of the series, it hangs on the wall, the shape of a bulging stomach. Inside, a red ovary is nestled, lit from within.

I touch my abdomen. My own red star radiates inside of me, glowing back at the sculpture, a pair of wretched twins.

At home, after the museum, I do another line. Then I open my laptop and search for clinics.

On the phone, a woman answers, kind and concerned.

"How far along are we?" she asks, as if we are in this together. Her voice is cloudlike. She sounds like she would be a nice mother. I imagine being raised by her, wrapped in a gentle, white mist.

"I'm not sure," I say.

"Well, we can help you figure that out once you get here," she says. "Now, have you already tested positive at home?"

"Yes," I say. "I saw two lines. There were two lines. The second line. I saw it. There was one line at first, but then the sec—"

She can tell I am unraveling and gently interrupts.

"Well, when can you come in, sweetheart? We should probably figure out how far along you are before we get into your options."

"Do you have time today?" I ask.

I realize I'm crying when the tears hit my mouth, salt stinging my lips.

"We sure do, sweetheart. Why don't you come down this afternoon? Let me get your name and number, and we'll get this train moving."

I answer her questions. Tears stream down my face. The black hole dilates wildly.

I am not sure what is happening to me, but I'm taking action. I am moving forward. The train is leaving the station.

I do another line and stare into space from my couch. For a moment, everything around me dissolves and I am suspended in a dark fog.

Then I gather myself. I tell myself it is just a task to complete. It is just an item on a to-do list.

I tap my phone screen. In two minutes, a car arrives. The conversation with the driver is minimal. The car smells of cheap soap, and nausea washes over me. The urge to vomit passes. The scene is like a movie again, no longer my life. It doesn't even need a sad soundtrack.

At the clinic, a group of women stand in a circle. They wear long skirts and raincoats with hoods, sensible shoes. Most have gray hair and wrinkled faces. As I near the entrance, one woman peels off from the group and approaches.

"You don't have to do this," she says. "I know how you've been lied to. There is time to make the right choice."

She holds a small pamphlet with the words *Your Mother Chose Life* on the cover and a set of black rosary beads. A thin white cross at the end of the strand trembles in the air.

Rosaries are crafted from rose petals in certain cultures. I saw it in a documentary: an old woman with spotted hands and coarse gray hair pulled into a loose bun boiled rose petals, then shaped them into small beads. A small bead of rose petals must look like an embryo.

"I'm only here for some tests," I say.

Her eyes flash in accusation. "You cannot lie to God. He sees all. He sees what you do."

But God isn't present in cities, I want to tell her. There isn't enough sky or space or time for God in the city. God can only exist in the country, where the sky is so big you can press your face against it, right up into the blue, until the light swallows your vision. That's one way to become a Believer.

When I was young, I thought God was a giant eye in the sky, spying on the world below. If God were a giant eye, could he see through my skin, down to the red petals in my womb? Would the giant eye know what happens next? Was the giant eye tied to the black hole?

"He sees all," the woman says, rubbing the rosary between her thumb and forefinger. "He knows what you are going to do! You'll be the one burning in hell for it!"

religion

/rəˈlijən/

noun

1. the belief in and worship of a superhuman controlling power, especially a personal God or gods.
2. a particular system of faith and worship.

e.g., I watched my parents pull away in our big yellow station wagon. My father had christened it the Banana Boat. They had dropped me off at catechism class. I was eight. Class was every Tuesday. For four hours, I'd learn about the Bible, surrounded by girls my age.

I waited in the church garden until the nuns called us in. Lush green ivy crawled up gray stones. That part felt a bit like magic to me, so I liked arriving early. There was a hush over everything. I thought that was called holiness.

The nuns wore starched black and white, brown crosses hanging from their necks. Their heads were covered, so we could not see the hair above their wrinkled faces. Their hands looked like the paws of the rats in my science book. They motioned us inside.

For the four hours, I sat, bored out of my mind, watching the white wall clock tick away the time with its black hands.

One Tuesday, a new nun was in the classroom. She may have

been more important because she wore a better outfit than the other nuns and had a bigger head covering.

"Let's welcome Sister Theresa to class this afternoon," a regular nun said. "She's here for a special presentation."

"Hello, children," Sister Theresa said. "Today, we're going to talk about your bodies and babies."

I imagined my stomach full of babies, a bunch of them moving around inside like hamsters. A shiver went up my spine.

"What's important, first, is that you only give your body to a man in the sanctity of the union of Catholic marriage," Sister Theresa said. "But I'm also here to tell you another important thing about your body."

We all waited to hear what the thing was. Sister Theresa reached for a bag on the desk.

"You might one day find yourself pregnant," Sister Theresa said. "And I want to talk about what happens when there is a baby in your body and why it is so important to God for you to keep that baby safe in your body."

She handed the bag to a girl in the front row. The girl bowed her head and took something out, then passed the bag back to the girl behind her, who did the same.

"A baby is a gift from God," Sister Theresa said. "A child is God's greatest creation and his holiest of treasures. It is our divine duty to bring forth children and to raise them in God's loving light."

The bag had made its way to me. I peered down.

Inside, there were dozens of tiny plastic fetuses. They were all crowded in there, their little bodies banging up against each other. Their skin was the color of mine. I took one from the bag like I was supposed to before I passed it to the next girl.

"Now, girls, what you hold in your hands is a baby at twelve weeks," Sister Theresa said.

I cradled the fetus in my palm. It was curled up, as if it were cold. It had small bumps for ears, and a tiny mouth. Its eyes were closed, as if it were sleeping.

"Under no circumstances should this baby be killed," Sister Theresa said. "Can we all agree on that?"

I looked around to see all the girls nodding along. I nodded, too.

"Now, there are people who will tell you that you can kill this baby and it won't matter," Sister Theresa said. "But this baby matters! Every baby matters to God!"

I thought of the big eye in the sky looking down at me and the fetus in my hand.

"I want you to take your babies home with you and protect them so that they grow strong and beautiful through God's love and your devoted care," Sister Theresa said. "Just as you will one day care for real babies after you marry."

I took the fetus home with me. That night, I laid it next to me in bed, as if it were mine, as if I were already a mother.

I nside, the clinic is painted light beige and the floor is lined with blue-gray industrial carpet. The carpet reminds me of my office. I squint at the floor and pretend I'm at work, not here.

"Are you here for an appointment, hon?" calls a voice.

Behind a wall of bulletproof glass, a blond nurse in scrubs and a pale blue surgical mask tilts her head at me from her desk, her blue eyes vibrant above the fabric covering the bottom half of her face. She is one of the few I've seen wearing masks. Looking around, I realize the entire staff is masked.

"Yes," I say. "I have an appointment at three."

"Let's get your paperwork started and we'll have you moving in no time," she says, sliding a clipboard through a slot.

I take note of her careful language, how she will not acknowledge the precise reason I am here.

I write down the facts of myself: address, medical history, age, insurance, emergency contact—Maria.

After a few minutes, the nurse escorts me to a small room with two chairs.

"Now, hon, we're just going to do some blood work here," she says. "We want to get everything confirmed before you meet with the doctor."

Then it unfolds: the preparation of my arm, the appearance

of the silver needle, the prick into the vein, blood coursing out of me into the vial, red, red, red, red as the inside of the pomegranate.

The nurse then escorts me to an examination room and vanishes with the vial. I sit on the table and the white butcher paper crinkles and tears beneath my weight. I hate the sound, so I hold my breath, try to keep still. The black hole hangs above the scale.

The doctor is a woman with chestnut hair and kind brown eyes above her mask.

"Hi, there," she says as she steps into the room, my chart in her hand. A giant engagement diamond perched on her finger flashes a rainbow prism on the wall. "How are you?"

"I'm okay," I say, finally out of tears. "How are you?"

"I'm good," she says with cheer.

Her joy catches on my skin, a piercing silver hook. She is good, maybe great, or at least better than I am. She is having a normal day. She probably kissed her husband goodbye before heading to work. Maybe she hummed along to her favorite song in the car on the way here. She is not staring down the barrel of a gun, not today.

"Now, I know you tested positive at home," she says, more subdued. "And I wanted to let you know that your blood work confirms that you are pregnant."

The news hits harder now, a sledgehammer to the heart, my gut twisting in on itself. The at-home test had some margin of error. I realize I'd been holding out hope the results were wrong, that I could still emerge from all of this unscathed.

"I . . . I see," I choke out.

"If you're comfortable with it, I think it would be good to discuss your options."

I see them: the women with the rosaries, the nun handing out the plastic fetuses, the man beneath my window, Maria, Nicole, the chef, my mother, my father, Sasha, the CEO.

"It doesn't feel like the best time to bring a child into the world," I say. "I can't give a child what it needs."

She nods in sympathy. It's the first time I've said any of this out loud.

"I think . . . I think I would end up being a single mother," I say.

I see: the chef at home with his girlfriend, my bills overdue, the anger and possible envy on Sasha's face when I tell her I am pregnant, my father's disappointment, my bright future replaced with another, darker path forward.

"The father isn't in the picture?"

"Not . . . not in any real way."

"Financially, could you . . . ?"

Another flash of a possible future: a child emerging from between my legs, blood everywhere, the cord like a cow's intestines.

"No, not in this city. It's a terrible place to raise a child. And a terrible time, for me."

"I understand," she says. "It's a hard decision, but we support you. Now we need to determine when your last period was, so we can figure out your options."

I tell her the date of my last period.

"That would put you at between six and seven weeks," the doctor says. "You'll need to make your decision soon, so we can get the procedure scheduled."

The procedure. The vagueness of the language scares me.

Another flash: a wrinkled newborn against my bare chest, tiny fingers curled, mouth to my nipple. I wait for my heart to respond to the image, but I feel nothing.

"At six weeks, to give you an idea, the embryo is about the size of a pomegranate seed," the doctor says, cupping her hand as if she is holding something very small and delicate. "We don't want to rush your decision. I just want to point out that the longer we wait, the higher the risk of complication."

I imagine: the doctor plucking exquisite fruits from my womb, presenting them to me when I wake up. I am filled with: dragon fruit, passion fruit, guava, figs, pomegranates.

"Obviously, you can wait longer," she says. "But it's better for you both if we do the procedure within the next few days."

For you both. Does she mean the chef and me? Or me and the child?

"Okay," I say. "I would like to have the procedure."

"We'll get you scheduled," she says. "We know this is never easy, but we are here for you."

This is never easy. What does she mean by *this*? *This* means my mess, my life, the child I am not having. *This* means the fruit inside of me, removed.

"What will the process be like?" I ask.

"First we'll put you under twilight sedation."

"Twilight sedation?" I ask.

"We want to make sure you won't be in any pain. Don't worry, you'll wake up pretty soon after the procedure."

"How long will it take?"

"It will take about ten minutes, then we'll keep you under observation and send you home to rest once we give the all-clear. Most women experience pain for a few days, as well as spotting or heavy bleeding."

"I understand."

"You're going to be just fine," she says. "This is routine. And you are making the right choice for you. That's all that matters."

I cling to the word: *fine*. I try to make it true.

Before I leave, they give me a date and time. All the emotion is gone from me. It's all logic now, the completion of a task. I will need to take off work, I realize dully.

To calm myself, I construct the simplest scenario: in a few days, I will go to sleep and then I will wake up empty.

At home, on the sofa, in the late afternoon light. The strange sensation washes over me again: my body releases a flood of the hormone that tells me I want to be a mother. My heartbeat changes, the pulse in my ears whispers *mother, mother, mother*. I try to shake it off, but a protective hand goes to my belly.

The discount pomegranate sits on my counter. I pick it up. The fruit is deep red with hints of white and burgundy and yellow. It has a small crown at the top. I squeeze the pomegranate gently, unsure how to release the hundreds of seeds inside that glitter like bloody jewels.

I have dinner reservations with Maria and Nicole. Part of me wants to cancel, but I can't bear the thought of being alone with the black hole.

We meet at the tapas restaurant near my apartment. The walls are deep red, the rich color of the heart, and plastered in hip trash like car bumpers and cowboy boots sprouting fake flowers. The kitchen sent out a pair of octopus tentacles in the shape of a heart when I ate here with the chef a few weeks ago. That's how in love we looked.

Maria and Nicole are seated in the back, halfway through

a pitcher of sangria. Maria tugs at a curl. Nicole is in her black caftan, rolling her eyes.

"*Bitch!*" Maria says. Her brown eyes go electric when she sees me.

"Hey, girl," Nicole says, monotone. "Nice of you to show up."

"Sorry I'm late," I say, lying. "I lost track of time at the art museum."

"You're a space cadet," Nicole says.

"Oh damn, I wanted to catch that exhibit," Maria says. "Her work looks wild."

"It was fantastic, really weird and gruesome, in a way," I say. "Anyway, what do you two want to eat?"

The fake me takes over. I pretend I'm not nauseated. I keep my sad news buried. Some tombs have secret rooms. Inside of me, there is a dark cavern where my real self lives.

"Queso," Maria says. "And that octopus dish looks delish."

I see a possible future: I'm on a blood-soaked hospital bed, the chef's child tearing through me.

"That sounds perfect," I say. "I've been wanting to try it."

"So," Nicole says. "What's up with you?"

The end of her question has a prying point. I can feel the beak of it digging. Nicole is like my mother in this way: they both ask questions as if they're attempting to uncover a hidden vulnerability. They can detect shipwrecked secrets, like sonar under the waves. I wonder if she can tell I am pregnant.

"Nothing much! Just watching the world fall apart," I say. "Work's been crazy! They made me come into the office yesterday for some secret project."

"Of course they did," Nicole says.

The waitress approaches and we order.

"I had a panic attack yesterday when I got home from the office," Maria says. "I spent, like, four hours on my living room floor. I'm on a secret project, too, and it's too much to handle. Between work hell and rent increases and the virus, like, is this even a life?"

"I swear, you both act like you work for the fucking CIA," Nicole says, rolling her eyes. "Do I need a security clearance to hear about your day? And why are you two working on the weekends?"

"Yes," Maria says, eyes wide. "My NDA specifies that you need a certain level of access to the company. Please don't ask me any more questions. I'm prohibited from talking about it."

"How's the chef?" Nicole asks, homing in on one of my shipwrecks like a demonic radar technician.

"He's good, thanks," I say. I decide to give her a morsel. "He stayed the other morning and made me coffee. It was . . . different? But really nice."

"So, is he going to leave his girlfriend or what?" she asks. "Or are you two going to keep playing fantasy fuck house?"

"Relax," Maria says. "Let her have some fun in this hellhole. We all need something to get by here."

"This city is not a hellhole," Nicole says. "I have lived here for fifteen years, and it's an incredible place. The culture, the music, the food. You are both too new to appreciate what this city has to offer."

"Yesterday I saw a man shoot heroin between his toes and then smear his own shit on a store window," Maria says. "Explain that. Tell me that's incredible. You can't, you fucking can't."

Nicole starts to go off, but just then the waitress arrives with our drinks.

This shouldn't be a serious moment, but a blood orange

margarita now sits before me, the color of one thousand sunsets. It is more than tequila with salt around the rim. It is a choice, like the lines from my freezer.

Life splits like a snake's tongue. The two paths fork before me. Is this all life is? One choice followed by another, stacking upon themselves, until you are standing in your own future and you have become someone else?

I bring the glass to my lips and let the red-orange sweetness slide down my throat, into my belly, where the child waits, where it drinks the cursed sunset with me.

After dinner, we linger outside, in front of the restaurant. Maria passes around a vape pen with a hybrid THC in the cartridge, a strain designed to deliver the high without paranoia. Nicole takes long drags and exhales huge clouds. I wave the pen away when she passes it to me.

"What's up with you, Goody Two-shoes?" Nicole asks, a spark in her eye. "Too good to get high with us?"

"No, no, nothing like that," I say. "I have an early day tomorrow and I should head home soon."

"I don't want to go home," Nicole whines. "Let's go to another bar."

The thought of the night continuing, of drinking more alcohol, exhausts me down to my bones.

"I'd love to, but I have to pass."

"Me, too," Maria says. "I'm wiped out."

Nicole's pupils dilate, the clouds gathering within her before the storm.

"You know what I'm fucking sick of? You two. You two and

your fucking jobs. You're constantly overworking yourselves and buying into this tech hustle culture bullshit. At my job, we work like normal people."

"Our jobs?" I ask. "What do you mean? We have to work. That's the only way we can afford to be here."

"Oh, fuck off. You don't need to work ninety hours a week. You only like those jobs because they make you feel like you're better than me."

The winds of her storm pick up. I try to smooth things over.

"No, no, it definitely isn't that," I say. "We don't think we're better than you."

"Oh, fuck you both," Nicole continues. "You and your secret projects and your panic attacks."

"What?" Maria asks. "What the fuck did you just say?"

"We're just trying to get by," I say. "It's hard to live here."

It's the wrong sentence; as soon as the words leave my mouth, I know it is. Nicole rears back like an arm about to throw a hard punch.

"Hard to live here?" Nicole shoots back. "It's sooooo hard for you, huh? Soooo hard to be in this beautiful city and make six figures. Nothing is good enough for you two! *Nothing!* You're bottomless pits. You're ungrateful bitches! You're two black fucking holes!"

"Listen, you better watch your mouth when you talk to me, bitch," Maria says, her voice gone soft and scary. "Because it's going to get real wild out here if you keep going."

"*Me?* I'm the fucking problem? Not you two? I've fucking had it—you're both miserable fucks who need to get their heads on straight. *Get a fucking grip!*"

She howls the last part so loudly that it cuts through the

night like a fire alarm. Heads on the street turn. Humiliated, I stare down at the sidewalk. She's lost in the tantrum, there's no pulling her back with logic now.

Nicole, encouraged by the glances of onlookers, begins to stomp her feet, throwing her arms wide, screaming.

"You two don't like it here? Then leave! I don't need this shit!"

The scene is so chaotic that I can't stand another second of it. I walk away without Maria.

"Oh, classic Cassie! Just run away when things get hard!" Nicole calls after me.

I don't look back. I just keep moving forward.

I walk the few blocks home half drunk, the sting of Nicole's words still on me. Past the pastel buildings, past the stores that are shut down for the night or forever, and past the park, empty but for the lumps of bodies beneath filthy blankets.

I turn onto my block and come upon a scene: a police car flashes red and blue lights on the man who sleeps beneath my window. He sits on the sidewalk, hands cuffed behind him, two officers standing over him. They are talking, but I can't hear what they're saying.

As I open the front door, the man looks up and catches sight of me.

"*Well if it isn't the bitch!*" he says. "I know you did this! You call the cops on me? I bet you did, bitch!"

My hollow heart cracks.

"I didn't call the cops on you," I say, hanging my head as I step into the building.

"*Bitch, I bet you did!*"

Upstairs, I crawl into bed. The flashing lights vanish and the street beneath my window goes quiet, too quiet, quieter than it ever has been. I sob myself to sleep, the black hole hanging in the corner.

I dream I'm standing with the chef on an endless stretch of white sand next to the sea at twilight. I open my mouth to tell him about the baby, but he's already walking away, his back to me, as if I don't exist, as if I never have.

The horror of another Monday hangs over me the next morning. On the train, I check my phone and the headlines are worse than ever.

Rent Law Goes to Court

Wildfire Season Approaches

First Virus Death Confirmed in CA

I don't click the link. I saw it coming. We'll be like the other countries soon: sick, quarantined, dying.

On the train, I watch the sun rise in the clear sky, fantastic and electric. The beautiful weather seems wrong for how horrible the world is: my stomach full of child, the virus, the rent, the wildfires.

My phone chimes. A text from the chef:

Can I see you soon? I've been thinking a lot about you.

I tilt my head at my phone screen. He rarely asks to see me like this. A small, sparkling hope breaks through the darkness in my heart.

Of course! Later tonight?

I'm tempted to text him the phrase *I'm pregnant*, but decide against it. My phone lights up with his response. Panic cycles through my blood before I open his message: What if he says no? What if I am alone again tonight with the cells inside of me and the black hole?

Sure! Can't wait.

Relief dissolves my paranoia. Once I see him, it will all make sense. Once I see him, I will know my future.

"You're late," Sasha says.

"I caught the later train," I say.

"Why am I not surprised you're starting to slack off?" she says.

"Sorry. It's only 8 a.m."

She raises an eyebrow at me as if she might debate the meaning of time. "Did you write that offer letter yet? You know how important it is that you close this hire."

"I'm doing it right now."

"Well, hurry up. Every day, we're losing PR opportunities because you're not doing your job."

It is an awful task. It makes me sick. So my fake self takes over and writes the offer letter for Noor, detailing all of the pathetic specifics:

Home office: Lahore
Salary: $25,000

Signing bonus: $3,000
Stock options: $10,000

My fake self sends the offer letter to HR for approval. Then I slump down in my seat.

Another destruction meeting. The CEO, Jeremy, and Sasha all sit at the big conference table, their eyes tired. The sun shines through the windows and the palm trees outside shimmer green.

"Hey," Jeremy says coolly.

"Morning. How's it going?"

"Well, they hacked their way in last night," Sasha says. "Not that you'd know because you came in late."

"How did it go?" I ask.

"It worked," the CEO says. "The vulnerabilities were exposed. The data of three million users. Right now, we're focused on leaking the story. We need you to draft something for the hacker message boards."

"What?" I say.

"We're going to post about it and then the tech mags will pick the news up that way. Easier than giving a tip," Jeremy says. "We only need a few sentences from you."

The company speaks to me then, once again, but this time it tells the truth.

01011001 01101111 01110101 00100111 01101100
01101100 00100000 01101110 01100101 01110110
01100101 01110010 00100000 01110100 01110010
01110101 01101100 01111001 00100000 01100010

01100101 00100000 01101111 01101110 01100101
00100000 01101111 01100110 00100000 01110101
01110011 00101110 00100000 01011001 01101111
01110101 00100111 01110010 01100101 00100000
01101111 01101110 01101100 01111001 00100000
01101000 01100101 01110010 01100101 00100000
01100110 01101111 01110010 00100000 01100001
00100000 01100010 01110010 01101001 01100101
01100110 00100000 01101101 01101111 01101101
01100101 01101110 01110100 00100000 01100010
01100101 01100110 01101111 01110010 01100101
00100000 01110111 01100101 00100000 01100100
01101001 01110011 01100011 01100001 01110010
01100100 00100000 01111001 01101111 01110101
00101110 00100000 01000100 01101111 00100000
01111001 01101111 01110101 01110010 00100000
01101010 01101111 01100010 00100000 01100001
01101110 01100100 00100000 01100010 01100101
00100000 01110001 01110101 01101001 01100101
01110100 00101110 00100000

You'll never truly be one of us. You're only here for a brief
moment before we discard you. Do your job and be quiet.
We don't owe you anything. You are lucky to be along for
the ride. Don't ask questions. Don't speak. Perform. Produce.
Do what we tell you to do. You are nothing but a computer
with a pulse. We only want your motherboard. We are not
your friends. We are not your family. We are a team until we
have succeeded.

The silver glint of a headache flashes behind my eyes. The lights in the meeting room turn to halos.

"You can type it on my laptop," Jeremy says. "It's encrypted."

When he slides his laptop over, my fake self steps up and the words fall out of me.

Yesterday, data-reconciliation start-up Nomad suffered a DOM-based XSS attack. Nomad links website users to their bank accounts, so they can be targeted by third-party marketing. During the attack, a vulnerable endpoint was identified that exposed Nomad client data, putting the information of three million users at risk.

I pass the laptop back to Jeremy.

"Great," he says. "I'll use a masked IP to get this posted."

A terrible omen: an emergency meeting invite from the head of HR. His office is a fishbowl: three of the walls are made of glass so everyone can see inside. This is called transparency, one of the six pillars of our company culture, according to the poster on his only wall.

He sits across from me with his hands tented. He has a bland face and a half-zip with the company logo, earned after six years of service.

"Cassie," he says kindly. "How *are* you today?"

"Couldn't be better," I say. "How are you?"

"Good, good. But we do have something to talk about."

"Okay."

A montage of the potential mistakes I could have made: Sasha's complaints about my poor performance, a website I shouldn't have visited, using social media on company time.

"I noticed an issue in your offer letter to Noor in Pakistan."

Relief cools my panic.

"Oh? What's the problem?"

"Well, you hired him to work out of the Lahore office. But we don't have a Lahore office."

"What?"

"Our Pakistan office is in Karachi."

A beat passes.

"How far is that from Lahore?" I ask.

"About fifteen hours," he says.

"But Sasha said our Pakistan office was in Lahore."

The head of HR pauses. "Why would she tell you the office was in Lahore?"

"I have no idea," I say. "She was adamant that the role was based there because we had an office there."

A sympathetic look crosses his face. "I understand. I'm sorry for the confusion here. These mix-ups happen sometimes."

He gives me a weak smile. The smile says: *I have seen Sasha make a mess before.* The smile says: *she is a moron.* The smile says: *you are going to have to take the fall on this one.*

The black hole rises up next to him and expands, spinning angrily next to the table at the injustice.

"So let's move past blame and find a solution. Noor seems like a great candidate who would be an asset to VOYAGER. But obviously, we cannot extend him an offer to an office that doesn't exist."

"What do you want me to do? Cut him loose and hire someone in Karachi?"

"We've already made a verbal offer, so that's not on the table."

"Wait, we're still going to hire him?"

"I'd just like you to have a conversation with Noor. I want you to see if he is open to relocating to Karachi."

"But his family is in Lahore. He didn't sign up to move."

"How excited is he to work here?"

"Over the moon. Like he's won the lottery."

"Well, why don't you just suggest he relocate? Just test the waters here. See what his appetite is for the opportunity."

"Will we pay for the relocation? I mean, his salary is already so low. We can at least do that."

"We're not interested in footing the bill for that."

"Seriously?"

"Take his temperature on this, okay? See how he feels about relocating to Karachi."

"Can't I offer him anything for the move? Anything at all?"

"Tell him we'll cover the cost of his boxes."

"His boxes?"

"Yes, his boxes and supplies."

"But that's nothing. Like two hundred dollars."

"Best I can do. See how he feels about it and let's go from there?"

The head of HR shoots me a smile and stands up to indicate the meeting is over.

———

The news spreads from the hacker message board within hours. Headlines pop up on the major tech blogs and three newspapers pick up the story by the afternoon.

Nomad Puts the Data of Millions at Risk

Were You Compromised? Nomad Data Hacked

Here's What to Do if You Are a Nomad Customer

Even with the spread of the virus, we've managed to grab attention.

The CEO sends an opaque email of thanks. Later, in the kitchen, Jeremy nods at me with a gleam in his eye. It isn't from lust or love or promise of something to come. Instead, his green eyes shine from power.

Suddenly, it becomes so clear that I can't believe I didn't see it before: he is now one of the young gods. He has joined the pantheon.

I call home after the headlines hit. Outside, I stare numbly at the bay, at the bare backs of bathing men.

As the phone rings, I pretend they are men on a camping trip, men who have chanced upon a pristine lake. Sometimes reality hurts so badly we must twist it in order to go on living beside it.

The worst happens: my mother answers my father's cell phone. The black hole spirals slowly next to me, listening in.

I picture her there, in the kitchen, standing on the faded beige tiles, the house slowly going out of date around her, her face sinking into itself with the passing of time.

"How *are* you?" she asks, stretching the word out like an accusation.

"Good, good," I say.

I shove my truth down into a dark box, where it squirms, blind. There are caves in New Zealand where bioluminescent worms make nests of silk. The strands hang over the heads of visitors, dotted with glowing larvae. The truth is like that: buried and glowing in a cave you must travel far underground to enter, if you are brave enough, if you can face the darkness and step into its waiting mouth.

"Well, I'm great," my mother says. "I just got my nails done, and I'm about to go to a tapas bar to meet the girls. Have you ever had tapas?"

"Yes," I say. "I have had tapas. But should you be going out with this virus going around?"

"Aren't tapas the greatest? Small plates! Cute little bites. Me and the girls can't get enough of them! Do you and your friends ever get tapas? You never tell me about you and your friends."

She moves past the question. Instead, she focuses where she can hurt, where she can sting. Her tone implies my friends are lies, little fictions. But maybe they are. Maybe our lives are the lies we choose to tell each other.

"Yep," I say. "We had tapas last night as a matter of fact. But it's a little weird out here with the virus. Aren't you worried about it?"

"Oh, not in the suburbs," my mother says. "That's a city problem, you know. Anyway, how is your love life? Your father says there's a man."

My stomach twinges. I swear I can feel a baby kicking inside of me, even though I know there is only a small white clump of cells.

"Good, good," I say. "I've been seeing a guy. He's nice. He's sweet."

"It's crazy you don't ever tell me these things. Me, your mother. Your own mother. Well, all I'll say is don't mess it up this time," she says. "You know how you like to do that. You've always been that way with boys, even when you were little."

I count to three with my eyes closed. I imagine a green meadow with a crystal-clear stream, volcanoes erupting hot red lava, the ocean folding the coastline back up into itself, lightning ripping out of the sky and striking the ground of an empty midwestern field.

"How are the girls?" I ask. "You sound excited for dinner."

"Oh, good, you know. Michelle is getting a boob job."

"Good for her," I say. "She'll be so happy."

"I know, I know. And Gina got a Lexus. I told your father I want a Lexus."

"We're not getting a fucking Lexus," I hear my father say in the background.

I imagine him at the kitchen table, surrounded by his newspaper, glaring at her through his smudged reading glasses, his face red at the mention of money.

"I work hard! I should have a Lexus!"

"Your car is fine! You don't need a Lexus!"

"Nobody told me thirty-five years ago that I was marrying a cheap ass!"

"I have to get back to work," I say. My headache is full blown. "Can you put Dad on real quick?"

"*She wants to talk to you!* I love you," she says.

"Love you, too."

"Say it like you mean it!"

"Love you, too!"

"Hey, snookums," my father says.

"Hey, Daddio."

"How is it out there in beautiful sunny California? It's cold as hell here today, rainy, too. Be glad you're out there."

"It's good here," I say. "Some high-pressure work stuff, but that'll be over soon."

"Well, pressure means you're not expendable. You want them to believe you're necessary. Show them you're necessary, like I told you."

"Not expendable, not at all," I say.

I am standing on the edge of something, a future that will descend upon me soon, and I worry it will change things between us. For a moment, I want to confess everything to him, as if he is a priest, as if only he can absolve me.

"You good otherwise?" he asks.

"I'm okay."

"Well, we're all good here minus the great Lexus debate. I'm just getting older every minute."

"Stop it!"

"I'll be fertilizer in no time!"

"Dad!"

"Look, if God wants to take me, then let him. Beam me up, Scotty."

"You're not funny."

"Then why are you laughing? Anyway, let me get back to it here. Your mother is giving me that bitchy look. Love you."

"Love you, too."

I put away my phone. I stand in the ache of fresh silence, all my secrets caught in my throat.

bittersweet

\ˈbitər͵swēt \

noun
1. being at once bitter and sweet.
2. pleasure accompanied by suffering or regret.

e.g., On the day I flew to California for good, my father drove me to the airport. It was a cool spring day, the kind my father loved. Outside, the trees that edged the highway were tall and green, and the sun shot through the car windows, sparkling.

"You ready to be a California girl?" my dad asked. "Big day, big day."

I was terrified, my hard heart curled up into itself in my chest, burrowed like an animal. I wasn't sure how to feel—it was all happening so quickly. The black hole that day hung in front of the windshield above the dashboard, the size of my heart.

The packed boxes, the emptied apartment, the goodbye drinks with a few friends in a crowded bar. I'd moved through the town like a ghost for weeks—it didn't matter whom I touched or what I did, this phase of my life had ended. California beckoned with its sun and palm trees and the promise of a new career.

And here it was, then, us in the car to the airport. My father drove fast, but stopped so I could get a coffee. He wore a yellow rubber raincoat even though there were no clouds in the blue sky. Fathers did things like this: they gave advice and wore embarrassing outfits and sneakers and drove us to airports to begin our new lives.

"I'm ready, Daddio," I said. "I wonder what I'll be like when I get there."

"You'll be you but better," he said. "That's how people grow. We push ourselves into new places and then we change."

"But what if I don't want to change?"

"You have to change someday, honey bun. We all do."

Then he put a bittersweet song on the radio, something crooning and full of yearning, and I let the silence settle between us.

Later, I would cry at the airport when he hugged me goodbye. Later, I would cry quietly behind my sunglasses as the plane took off. Later, I would land in a new city and open the door to another empty apartment. Later, I would unpack my life and become another version of myself.

But for a moment, I stopped worrying because I was there, in the car beside my father, in the sun. For a moment, life stopped, and we were just there, together, listening to a sweet sad song on the highway.

"You're going to get out there and never look back," my father said over the strains of the song.

"You know it," I said.

But I wasn't so sure. The thought of it made an ache swell through my body. Tears gathered in my eyes and made the sunshine more dazzling. I turned my face to the window so he couldn't see my wet face. It hurt. But I crystallized the moment. I put it in the glass jar inside my heart.

Noor's hopeful face fills my screen. It's nighttime again for him, and he is in his bedroom. He looks energized, excited, electric. I realize this is what Sasha wanted from me when she extended my offer.

"Hello, Cassie!" Noor says. "So good to see you again!"

"You, too, Noor. Thank you for jumping on the call with such short notice."

"Well, anything for VOYAGER. I was wondering when I should expect to receive the written offer."

"That's what I wanted to talk to you about, actually."

"Oh?"

My fake self takes over and pushes forward.

"Unfortunately, there was a miscommunication. We are still so excited about you joining VOYAGER, but the role will no longer be based in Lahore."

He squints. "If not in Lahore, then where?"

"The role will be working out of Karachi. That's where our main office is."

My fake self just says it. I cannot believe it. The black hole rises up behind my laptop, ballooning.

"But Karachi is so very far away from my family," Noor says. "I would have to leave my whole life here behind."

"I know, and that's why I wanted to take some time to talk through this."

"So, I would move to Karachi?" he says, as if trying out the future on his tongue.

"Yes, and we would cover the cost of your moving supplies."

He falls silent. I can see his mind working: a big move, leaving his family, an entirely new city, the expenses. The black hole rotates, its scent filling the room with metallic sweetness.

"Just the supplies?"

"That is what we are prepared to offer at this time, in addition to your salary, signing bonus, and stock."

I can feel myself burying the truth of the stock. I can feel myself becoming one of them.

"I see."

"We believe you are the ideal candidate for this role, and we are so excited to have you here."

His face transforms, his excitement slowly returning. But it's a different kind, more subdued. I can tell he no longer trusts me.

"I am dedicated to VOYAGER," he says, as if to convince himself. "I will do anything for this company. So yes, yes, Cassie. I will move to Karachi for VOYAGER. I will show you I am the best person for this job and that no one will work harder for you."

The call ends. The screen goes blank. The fake me fades away. I sit with the terrible truth: I have tricked Noor into changing the entire trajectory of his life for nothing. The black hole moves closer and I stare into its depths as if it is a mirror that will reveal what I really am.

———

That night, there is a knock at the door, his knock. The black hole expands at the sound. There is red wine on the counter, two glasses. I am queasy and tender, but I want to be held.

I open the door and he's standing there with sparkling eyes, wearing a crisp button-down in a navy-and-red paisley pattern, the cuffs rolled up. He has a paper box in his hand. His beard is freshly trimmed.

"There you are," he says, his voice soft.

He pulls me close and our mouths meet. We are still our own world spinning on its axis when we are together.

We step into the kitchen and he sets the box of doughnuts on the counter. Then he picks up the pomegranate. The black hole draws closer to us, widening, spinning.

"What are your plans for this?" he asks.

"I'm not sure," I say. "I honestly don't know what to do with it."

He squeezes the fruit, testing the firmness.

"Well, it's got a few days left before you get nothing from it at all. Where are your plates? I don't want to make a mess."

I pull a plate from the cabinet and a knife from the drawer. He sets the pomegranate on the plate.

"Here's a technique I learned from another chef," he says. "Works like magic. Watch this."

He scores the skin of the fruit, at the top, near the small crown. The pomegranate weeps from the slits, burgundy juice running onto the white plate like blood. The black hole suddenly begins to let out its long, endless hymn. It's never sung when I'm with someone else. I stare at it, startled.

"This is my favorite part," he says, and twists his wrists. "There's so much you can do with a fruit like this."

The pomegranate skin splits open in three places, and wet, red seeds burst forth. It gives birth to dozens of glistening children. There is a violence to it. The black hole sings louder, a deafening hum that warbles. It's almost impossible to hear the chef over the sound.

"Here," he says, scooping some seeds up. "Try them."

He brings three ruby seeds to my lips. I open my mouth and let them fall onto my tongue. I bite and red juice escapes from my lips and runs down my chin. The black hole moves above us and widens. I swallow, sending the arils down to the child, our child.

I pour two glasses of wine. We entwine our legs on the couch.

"So how have you been?" he asks. "It's been a few days since I've seen you."

The time frame stings for some reason: it must have been years, a decade, a millennium since I've seen him. I can't find the words.

"Busy!" I say. "Work today was crazy. How about you? What are you going to do about this virus?"

Even worse, my body wants him. Despite the pregnancy, despite all the horrors of the world, a slow heat burns. His hand finds my bare thigh. The black hole watches us from the corner, wide and angry.

"You know, we're not sure yet. For now, everyone is using a lot of hand sanitizer and we're just watching the news. But I have more exciting things going on."

"Oh," I force myself to ask, anger rising in my chest. "What do you have going on?"

"Today I created a new edible fog that floats over an edible moss," he says. "That way when you eat, your fork is surrounded by an essence of the flavor before you actually experience the flavor."

"What's the flavor?"

"I want something clean, so it's going to be lychee."

I pretend to listen. But my gaze drifts to the black hole. Maybe there are multiple paths, multiple timelines, multiple dimensions.

Dimension One: Without a word, I straddle him, pull my dress up, and feel him go hard. We move into the bedroom, and the symphony plays again, those golden sounds, like hymns in a cathedral. Our illusion remains intact. The fantasy of a future for us continues.

Dimension Two: I turn to him and say, "We should talk." His face sours. I explain what is happening inside of my body. The news makes him forget, for a split second, to be a good man. He buries his face in his hands. He lets out a small moan. I will never be able to forget that, the instant he says the words: "God, no, fuck." Then he remembers himself and puts a hand on my leg. He says the right things: "What can I do to help?" or, "Do you want me to go with you?" and maybe I let him. But it is the beginning of the end. The mirror shatters.

Dimension Three: We are together, in a backyard, our little girl laughing in the sun. We are holding hands, watching her, and she is perfect, with brown hair and round cheeks, lips little pink valentines.

"Momma," she shouts. "Come look!"

She lifts her perfect arm, where a black-and-yellow caterpillar sits on her perfect palm. It slinks across her skin.

"It tickles," she says.

"It's going to become a butterfly," the chef says. "But it has to change first."

I see them together, and my heart becomes pure, white light. But above our child's head, a dark dot expands—she has her own black hole.

"Hey! Hey. Where'd you go?" the chef asks. "I lost you for a second there."

I smile weakly. I caress his face. Everything in the world can betray you.

"Just thinking about work stuff," I say. "You know how I get."

He cups my face and looks deep into my eyes.

"Today I was thinking about you," he says.

"Oh, were you?" I ask. Suddenly, there is a small tight bud of hope in my chest.

"I just wanted you to know that you are singular to me," he says.

Singular: from the Middle English, meaning *solitary*, *single*; also: *beyond the average*. It sounds like a romantic compliment, but it means nothing. It is a hollow word.

Everything is different now, but I want to pretend it is the same. I choose the first dimension. My fake self takes over and lifts her dress and straddles him. She knows exactly what to do and she does everything he likes.

I watch from above as they move against each other. The black hole watches, too. Maybe we are one and the same now, hovering above my fake self and the chef as they writhe.

Suddenly I understand the situation fully: there are multiple truths, but one truth is larger. He cares about me. And he can't give me anything real. I am worth something, but not enough.

Life's greater truth is like that, always there, waiting to slide its knife into the heart of our illusions.

When I wake in the morning, he is gone. I am alone again as always. My belly feels swollen with our child. It weighs me down as I move through the apartment. He didn't even notice the physical change in me. A flame of anger flickers, adding to the pain of managing everything myself, to the pain of being left with nothing.

I send an email to call out of work. I know Sasha will be furious, but I have no choice.

I open the blinds to a smoky apricot sky. I can barely see below to the street. I check my phone and read the headlines:

California Wildfires Devour Hundreds of Acres

CA Governor Bans Large Gatherings

Rent Protests Continue at Capitol

I click on the link about the wildfires.

Due to hazardous air conditions, authorities ask that you not leave your homes unless you are experiencing a medical emergency or are in a mandatory evacuation zone. In

addition, health officials urge all those in outdoor spaces to
wear masks to protect themselves.

Am I experiencing a medical emergency? I must be. I do a line. On the counter, the insides of the pomegranate are shriveled. I slip three seeds onto my tongue and let them slide down my throat. This time, I feed myself.

I tap my phone screen to call a car. I lock my front door on the way out.

In the stairwell, there is a small woven basket holding a few blue surgical masks next to a note from one of the neighbors: Be safe out there.

I slide the mask over my face. Then I pretend I'm just on my way to run an errand. I pretend this is someone else's life.

betrayal

/bəˈtrāəl, bēˈtrāəl/

noun

1. the action of betraying one's country, a group, or a person; treachery.
2. the action of betraying one's self or one's own best interests.

e.g., You can convince yourself of anything and keep on pretending for as long as you live. That's how a belief begins its evolution into faith. Faith is a belief in the unseen, a wholehearted hope that what you believe without proof is indeed true.

To love the chef was like religion in that way. As we grew closer, I chose to believe that his girlfriend did not factor into what was blooming between us like a thousand acres of cherry trees.

It was torrential, how quickly we filled each other up. Intellectually, he met me where I was. There was affection, there was romance, there was tenderness, and above all there was a passion so evident that once an old woman passing us on the street as we kissed whispered "lovers" at us, as if she was compelled to give name to what she had witnessed.

———

e.g., One day I took the chef to my favorite store, a high-end oddities shop. I led him inside by the hand and watched his eyes light up.

There were fossils and rocks and animal bones and peacock feathers and bottles holding preserved hearts. There were old leather-bound books and drawers of teeth. Everything was arranged as if we were in a history museum: shelves of skulls, cases of nautilus shells, a table of gigantic crystals that thrust long, shimmering arms into the air.

He squeezed my hand and his eyes went round. It was like seeing him as a child. He reminded me of my father in front of Lucy.

"I knew you'd love it," I said.

He dropped a soft kiss on my mouth, our lips grazing, but with a promise of more. We embraced beneath a wall of taxidermied heads: moose, deer, horse, giraffe, antelope, goat. The heads looked dignified, the eyes glassy and still. Churches have high ceilings to force you to look up, to make you feel a sense of reverence. I felt a sense of reverence then, as if we were standing under the stained glass saints lining the wall of a chapel.

The most terrifying of all was the head of a black goat, which had pitch-black eyes and spiraled horns.

"He's evil," the chef said, dropping my hand to take a picture. "He's perfect, though, isn't he?"

"He's the best," I said.

"He's like you," the chef said, and my heart took flight in my chest, a small winged beast.

He snapped photos, and I wandered over to a display of jawbones. I stared through the white and into the empty spaces where their red tongues had been. Looking back, it becomes clear: you have to betray yourself first in order for anyone else to betray you.

e.g., Of course, I looked her up. I searched, and I found her, the girlfriend. It was a way of hurting myself, and I did it on purpose.

In her profile picture, she had brown hair, blue eyes, full lips. A caption announced that she had paid for the lips, and the results were worth every penny. Her nose was sharper than mine. She looked more catlike. She looked as if she could have her cake and eat it, too. She looked perfect, flawless.

Other than that, we didn't look so different.

Outside, the streets are practically empty. The orange sky and the smoke from the wildfires make the scene apocalyptic, terrifying. A cold chill runs through me.

The man who lives beneath my window is awake, sitting cross-legged on a sleeping bag. His bare face is exposed to smoke and orange glow.

"Morning," he says.

"Morning," I say.

Next to him is a pile of fruit: bananas, apples, pears. The fruits are bruised and ordinary. They make me homesick.

"This place looks like hell," he says. "Doesn't it?"

"It does," I say.

For a moment, we stare out at the scene, at the world dying before our eyes, and we fall silent at the sadness of it all. There is a short list of great levelers: grief, trauma, fear. In our fear, for a moment, we become the same person.

Suddenly, I am overcome with emotion and tears gather in my eyes.

The car pulls up.

"Be careful out there," he says.

"You, too," I say.

Then I get inside, half me, half someone else already.

———

"Morning," the driver says.

"Morning," I say. The black hole slides in next to me, almost a comfort now, proof I'm not alone.

A beat passes before he asks.

"Where are you heading today? I don't recognize this address. Not sure you should be out and about right now, especially alone."

I typed the address in manually, so he wouldn't know the exact location. In the rearview mirror, our eyes meet above our masks. His brow is furrowed in concern. He seems kind, fatherly. A pang tears through my chest as my father's face glitches through my mind.

"I have a doctor's appointment I can't miss," I say.

"Okay," he says.

We make our way up and down the hills. The city is quiet beneath the rusty sky. The sun is a harsh red eye.

I rest a hand on my stomach. I wonder if the child can sense where we are going, can sense what is about to happen to it. Nausea grips me. I remind myself it isn't a child.

When we pull up to the clinic, there are more protesters than before. They are waving signs:

Jesus Loves Your Baby

Thou Shalt Not Murder

An Embryo Is a Person

The driver's eyes sharpen in the rearview mirror. Who I am is now clear to him.

"Good fucking luck," he says under his breath as I climb out of the car.

daughter

/ˈdôdər, ˈdädər/

noun
1. a girl or woman in relation to either or both of her parents.
2. a nuclide formed by the radioactive decay of another.

adjective
1. originating through division or replication.

e.g., Sometimes I miss my mother. Or maybe I miss the mother I didn't have. There is a void where a certain love should be, a different type of abyss. What rushes in to fill the space? Anxiety, doubt, a very specific melancholy. A steel wall has been built around the red of my heart when it comes to my mother. All of that red of me is trapped inside of metal, caught, kept.

Here are the facts: this is called a boundary. A boundary hurts just as much as being stung by my mother. Love is just as painful as its absence.

e.g., The last time I saw my mother, we went to the grocery store to buy steaks for my last dinner. My father would take me to the airport the next morning, then I would be in California, in my new life. Then I would be a new person.

The meat counter glowed blue beneath the white fluorescent lights above our heads. The cuts were precise. There were no heads or legs to assign to the pieces splayed out before us. The meat was marbled with fat, thin white lines ribboning through the deep red.

The butcher was young. He wore a black rubber apron over a white coat. There were telltale drops of blood on the white fabric. If I were a detective, he would be the prime suspect.

"We'll take your finest steaks," my mother said proudly. "My daughter is moving to California and we are celebrating tonight."

The butcher and I stood in the silence of no one having asked her for those details.

"Great," he said flatly. "What type of steaks do you want, exactly?"

My mother's face was warped and reflected in the glass between her and the meat, her and the bits of bodies we would eat later.

"Let's do sirloin," she said loudly. "Your father loves sirloin, doesn't he?"

I nodded. I hated sirloin. My father loved sirloin. But a man's needs trumped a woman's every time, I had learned that by then.

The butcher wrapped the meat in white paper and tied it with white string. The package of flesh was heavy in my hands. We navigated through the store, collecting a box of mashed potato flakes and a small white cake from the bakery before the cashier rang us out.

In the parking lot, my mother turned to me.

"You know, I don't love what you're doing with your hair," she said.

My hair was normal hair, hair that hung to my chin.

"My hair?" I repeated.

"Well, you have a round face, you have to admit it. Because you put on some weight. And so since your face is fat, your hair should be much longer. It will help to hide your chins."

I hadn't gained any weight. My face was my face was my face. My mind began to unravel a little, out there, on the asphalt, in the parking lot.

"My hair is fine as it is," I said quietly.

"What did you say?" my mother asked.

There was a curve in her voice. I knew the curve well. But I was tired of everything that came out of her mouth.

"I think my hair is fine as it is," I said a little louder.

"That's exactly what a fat girl would say," my mother shrieked, there in the parking lot, a few feet from the car. "And that's exactly what someone who doesn't trust her own mother would say."

A chorus of wasps descended on the scene. The first wave had already reached me and the stinging had begun. None of it made any sense, I hadn't done anything wrong. But that was never the point. I had to deflect.

"I do trust you," I said.

"No, you don't. You only trust your stupid father. The two of you, peas in a fucked-up pod."

Anger erupted across her face, a contortion to her mouth and eyes that terrified me, like the warning smoke coming off the top of a mountain. Sometimes the wasps gave way to a volcano.

"Well, you've got nothing to say?" she screamed. "So you admit it! You both hate me!"

Whenever my mother became a volcano, my father would say: *We're off to the races.*

"I didn't say anything like that," I said.

"*You didn't need to say it,*" my mother shrieked. "*You tell me every day by your actions!*"

She was so full of rage that I stepped back, away from her, afraid she might strike.

"Nobody is going to hit you, you wimp," she spat out.

But the rage was still simmering off her, and she still hovered close to me, within arm's reach, too close. Then she reached over and grabbed my arm, digging her nails into my skin.

"Say you don't hate me," she raged. "Say it now. I'm your mother, say it."

"I don't hate you," I said, flat and terrified. Her nails dug deeper. I thought I might start to bleed.

The sentence hung in the air. *Off to the races.*

"You ungrateful little bitch," she said, her jaw clenched tight, her eyes on fire.

All the years of stinging rose up within me and finally I shook her claws off my arm, forcefully, determined to stand up for myself.

She almost fell backward, but caught herself at the last moment.

"You abusive bitch," she shrieked. "Look at yourself. Look what you have become!"

My face flushed red and I disassociated. I looked down at my feet. In the scuffle, I'd dropped the grocery bag to the ground and the cake tumbled out onto the asphalt, its plastic dome cracking and spilling all the white sweetness and frosting onto the blackness.

We got into the car. My heart thudded in my chest the way the pulse of the earth might force a volcano to rush the blood of lava out of the open wound of the land. We sat in bitter silence. In the harsh quiet, I made a promise with myself to never be alone with her again.

e.g., Everything I knew of love was built on this crooked foundation. In our lives, we must hold two truths at the same time. And the same way I must hold the stinging and the eruptions, I must hold something else: a sweet memory of my mother.

We were in the kitchen. I was ten years old. Her favorite song, an Elton John song, came on the radio. She was heating up dinner in the microwave, the Salisbury steaks scenting the air.

When my mother was young, she would listen to Elton John on her record player, endlessly. She'd wear out *Goodbye Yellow Brick Road*. There in the kitchen, when the song came on, she got young again. She couldn't see herself like I could see her then, how bright she became. She pressed a hand over her heart in the kitchen and began to sway. She sang the chorus, she sang *AhhhhAhhhhhAhhhh* and it was beautiful to watch because she loved to belt that note so much, she sang it with beauty and with pain, all of the pain of her life coming out of her mouth in that note, she transcended herself and became the note, and I loved her most then, when she was that note, swinging, swaying, electric.

I must have crystallized that moment. I must have kept it in the glass jar inside of my heart.

The protesters are relegated to a zone six feet away from the door. Although they cannot touch me, they yell, and some wave their rosaries in my direction.

The protesters remind me of the nuns: gray hair, wrinkled, older. They look garish when they scream at me with the thick smears of their wide, dark pink mouths.

"You are murdering God's creation," one woman says.

My breath quickens under my mask.

"You do not have to do this, but if you do, you will burn in hell."

Hell, with its demons and flames and eternal torment. What is the sin? My deliberate steps to the clinic or my work with the CEO or the affair with the chef? I can't tell which sin sends me to hell.

The black hole hovers over my right shoulder as if protecting me and trails me inside.

The clinic is silent, almost peaceful. The same nurse sits behind the plastic partition. She raises her head when she sees me, her blue eyes sweet above her mask.

"You're here for your 1 p.m. appointment, honey?" she asks.

"Yes," I say.

If I close my eyes, I could be in a hair salon. If I close my eyes, I could be anywhere but here.

"We'll take your payment now. It's better to do it now than to wait until after," she says.

"Payment," I repeat.

"Well, yes, hon. Let me check here. For your procedure, the fee is $750."

The number is a punch in the gut. I barely have enough to cover it, and I won't see another paycheck for two weeks.

I slide my credit card and hold my breath, but the light beeps green and the screen says *Approved*.

The nurse nods. Her demeanor is too sweet, too soft, a kindness I do not deserve. Maybe I deserve the screaming outside, the harshness of their judgment. I follow her to a room at the end of the hall.

"Now, if you'll please strip down and put on the gown," the nurse says. "The doctor will be with you shortly and we'll take real good care of you."

All I know of the world is a pane of glass and the baby inside of me is a brick right through it.

The cold air pimples my skin when I undress. The robe is thin and scratchy. I sit on the bed, crinkling the butcher paper again. A cheap framed photograph of peonies in a vase hangs on the wall. I stare into their soft pink faces, those paused pale fireworks.

I hear a knock before the doctor enters.

"How are we feeling today?" she asks, her brown eyes sparkling above her mask, her engagement diamond still sparkling on her finger. It is hard to keep track of whether we are wearing the masks for the virus or the fire.

"A little sick," I say. "Nervous."

"All normal feelings for what's happening right now. I'm going to take you down to a room where we'll sedate you. While you're under, I'll remove the cells. When you wake up, we'll be all done. It's that simple."

I follow her into the new room. Next to a bed with screens around it, another masked woman stands with scrubs on.

"This is your anesthesiologist," the doctor says. "I'm going to perform an ultrasound before she sedates you."

I nod and climb onto the table and straighten my gown. I stare up at the ceiling, then direct my eyes to another cheap framed photograph. This time, it is a field of red tulips hanging on the wall. The black hole floats to the right of the plastic gold frame.

I touch my stomach one last time and gauge the turmoil there. My rage is gone, the volcano dormant.

I focus on the tulips as the doctor smears gel over my belly. I am learning peacefulness by lying still, I tell myself. She's just going to let the air in, I tell myself.

"Now, we're going to hear a sound like a heartbeat," the doctor says. "So this might feel emotional. But it is not a heart-beat, per se—it's the fluttering of the cluster of cells inside of you where the heart would begin to grow."

Cluster of cells. I was wrong to call it a baby. It was too soon for that. I keep my eyes locked on the tulips as the doctor locates the cells. I don't know if I want to pray or weep. I am a ripe fruit that will be made to spill its seeds. *She's just going to let the air in.*

Then, a small sound: the fluttering. She's right, it sounds a bit like a heartbeat but not quite. For a moment, I break away from the flowers and look directly at the screen: a black-and-white blur where the cells have clustered inside of me.

I look closer and see my worst fears confirmed: floating next to the blur is a small black hole, almost impossible to see except it expands and then contracts. My black hole floats over to the screen as if to see its own child.

I picture the downy hair of my child with a black hole haloing its head, and it is then that I weep.

"Are you sure you want to proceed?" the doctor asks gently. "I have to ask one more time."

I nod and turn back to the tulips in the frame. Instead of being the body on the table, I walk among the bobbing red heads of the flowers as the nurse slides the needle into my arm. I am a riddle in nine syllables. I have boarded another train that is leaving the station.

As the drugs work through my veins, I chant quietly to calm myself.

She is just going to let the air in, she is just going to let the air in.

Then the tulips become a red river rushing out of the picture frame, a current of scarlet petals carrying me away, to a land of purple twilight, a land without the child.

A distant fire of pain roars through my abdomen, waking me. The drugs keep the pain at arm's length, but it still thrums dully through my empty womb.

The masked face of the anesthesiologist hovers above me, her eyes hazel and warm.

"You did great," she says softly. "You're going to be groggy for a bit."

The room is cold. On the wall, the once vibrant tulips suddenly look fake. Their glow is gone. My head is cloudy. I touch my stomach. It still feels hard, but there is a new tenderness and I know it is hollow.

The doctor appears and asks me to get dressed, using a voice one uses to address the fragile. It takes me a moment to realize I am the fragile one, a woman made of glass.

They bring in my discharge paperwork. I look it over with the black hole levitating next to me.

"When can I go back to work?" I ask.

"Tomorrow," the doctor says. "But please take it easy."

I imagine myself back at the office, carrying the pain with me silently.

Very slowly, I step through the clinic doors. Outside, the protestors resume their screaming, their eyes ablaze, their faces like wet petals smeared on a canvas. I cross the street to get away from them and wait for my car to arrive.

The sky is even more orange. The black hole hovers up high, next to the strange sun burning through the smoke, two eyes watching over me: one red, one black.

At home, my body is weak and trembling. Sharp cramps work their way through me as the drugs begin to wear off. They are a dull scream from another reality, another universe, another dimension.

I take the painkillers they've given me, then fall into bed. The drugs make the hours bleed into each other, time smearing itself against me. My sorrow is so deep it feels as if my chest might cave in. The silence eats away at me until I pick up my phone and dial the chef.

"Hello?" he answers.

"Hi," I say.

"What's going on?" he asks. "Everything all right? You never call."

"Had a hard day and wanted to hear your voice," I say.

"That's sweet of you," he says. "Been a crazy day here, too! Trying to balance our books—the dinner reservations are down because of the virus."

"Yeah?" I ask.

"Yeah, it's a mess. Maybe we just start building out a to-go menu? I don't know."

"That's really smart . . ."

"Oh! I forgot to tell you! I took my girlfriend to that store you showed me—the one with all the crystals and bones?"

The world stops. My shoulders tremble. I have to summon the fake me to make it through this conversation. She is exhausted, but she takes my place onstage.

"Yeah?"

"Yeah! Oh, she *loved* it! We had the best time exploring."

"Oh . . . I'm so glad."

"And guess what?"

"What?"

"We bought one of those freaky heads! We got the black goat, you remember him?"

"Yeah, he was gorgeous," the other me says.

"We hung it up in our living room," he says. "It's so badass. I'll text you a picture."

"Cool," she says.

"Anyway, I have to get back on the line. See you in a few days, okay? Wish me luck."

"Good luck."

I fall back into my bed. My phone dings. The photo: the black goat head above a green velvet sofa. It is another knife to the heart. The black hole keeps watch as I fall asleep, aching and alone.

A woman shouldn't be seen like this, all ruined. Or maybe everyone should have to see me, all of them, especially the men, the aftermath, the knives in their hearts for once.

I open my eyes and I am on an almost empty train: unshowered, same clothes from the clinic, a headache, a scathing fire in my empty womb. I can smell my own bad breath behind my mask. I can't remember how I got here.

Through the fog of pain, a new development: the black hole floats above my head now. At first I can't find it, but when I look up, it expands, a new dark halo.

I check my email, and there is a message from the CEO. The subject line: *Our Office Is Not Closed, Mandatory Report In.*

Outside, the sky is choking on its own orange, the sun a raging red over the silver bay. The water glints like knives.

I look up into the belly of the black hole. The abyss is so dark that my eyes begin to play tricks on me, casting colors up into the darkness.

When I tear my eyes away from the black hole, reality warps around me. For a split second, everything glitches and I can see inside all the Believers on the train, through their skin and chests, down into the cavities of their rib cages where their hearts beat, but their hearts aren't red, they are black, dark as the abyss.

Above their heads, I see my child bathed in a golden light, laughing in another dimension. The mirage is exquisite in its

mania: bright, warm, tender. I look down at my own chest, which
is nothing like theirs. Beneath my shirt and my skin, my red heart
bangs against my ribs, a wild animal ready to break free and gnash
its teeth at the throat of the world.

The big conference room is a morgue, but no one else rec-
ognizes it. No one else can see what I can see. The CEO, Sasha,
and Jeremy sit at the table with their laptops and seltzers.

"You look like shit," Sasha says, but she sounds muted, under-
water. "I can't believe you thought the office was in Lahore. You
need to pay more attention. I shouldn't have to figure out everything for you."

I can feel the earth rotating beneath my body, and all the
galaxies above me revolving, colliding, combining stars and dust,
dark matter merging.

"Let's stay on track," the CEO says. "I'd like new ideas."

With that, I wait for my fake self to take over. I even call for
her: *Where are you?* But nothing happens. *Where are you?* The
question echoes, as if I am calling into an empty cave, my fake
self long gone. The black hole expands above me. It widens to
blot out the ceiling above us.

Now the conference room is a screen I could punch through.
What would be beyond the surface? My new knowing reveals
the truth beneath the illusion. The CEO, Jeremy, and Sasha age
before my eyes.

Their faces wither, their eyes yellow, their hair goes gray, their
jaws slack, their lips thin and disappear. I see through all their
layers: skin, muscle, bone. They are already dead, only black blood

pulsing through their veins, their black hearts glistening like fat maggots.

"She seems spaced out today," Jeremy says, but his voice sounds warbled. "Did you sleep all right?"

Another glitch and reality wavers again. Suddenly I can see into Jeremy's future, crystal clear and shimmering above his head, everything he has been working against for his whole life coming to fruition. Years from now, he is potbellied, old, sitting on a sunken couch in a suburban home watching television, a faceless wife shrieking his name from the kitchen.

"She's not consistent. See what I've been saying? I put that in her performance review," Sasha says, her voice distorted. "Cassie, hello? We're talking to you."

Sasha's future dances above her head, a horrible hallucination only I can see: her face is sunken, wrinkles finally overtaking the injections, and she sits hunched at her kitchen table, at home, alone, the house soundless, no children, her body finally collapsing in on itself.

"Cassie?" the CEO says. "I said ideas. Now."

The CEO's future is perhaps the most terrifying. A vision of his life comes into focus above his head, and I can see him, on a sidewalk, homeless, begging, the inverse of his life's mission.

I remember the words of a physicist: *Anything that can happen will happen.* What we resist the most is eventually what must befall us. What we fight eventually becomes our future.

The black hole rotates above us, bigger than it has ever been. A hymn begins, a beautiful symphony of gravitational notes, a song made for me. It is a summoning.

A tidal wave of peace washes over me; I feel a rush of power, of decisiveness, of calm. I stand up and leave the conference room, ignoring Sasha as she calls after me. A golden path unfolds before me. A new purpose emerges. A thousand flowers bloom. A bright white light shines in the center of the darkness.

I run down the stairs and out the door into the orange haze. Outside, the men are standing in the bay, more of them than ever, dozens of them now, washing in the water.

I look back at the mirrored office complex for the last time. The men in the water are warped reflections in the glass of the building. I picture it: holding a match to the long fuse of a bomb and the building exploding. I let the flames roar behind me, and I swear I can feel the heat at my back as the whole wretched place burns to the ground, like the trees in the wildfires, like the man who set himself on fire in the street silently screaming from the center of the white-hot flames.

singularity

/ˌsiŋgyəˈlerədē/

noun

1. the state, fact, quality, or condition of being singular.
2. a point at which a function takes an infinite value, especially in space-time when matter is infinitely dense, as at the center of a black hole.
3. a hypothetical moment in time when technologies have become so advanced that humanity undergoes a dramatic and irreversible change.

e.g., A singularity is a region of infinite density, where the laws of space and time as we know them cease to exist. It is the ultimate no-man's-land where all matter is compressed down into an immeasurably tiny point.

e.g., I am alone in my train car on the way home. Once we reach my stop, I make my way through the empty station. There are no more crowds, no more mothers pushing strollers, the blind violin player is long gone.

Outside, the sky is a dark, violent orange. The streets are almost entirely deserted.

I soon arrive at a place I remember: the same place where the man set himself on fire, the sidewalk where the air was sucked from his contorted mouth as the flames licked at his skin.

I expect to see a burn mark on the ground, some sign that he was here, but by now, all the evidence is gone. The world has moved on. A deep sadness echoes through me, colored with exhaustion.

e.g., The black hole descends to face me. It swells larger and larger alongside my sadness, until it blots out the sun, filling the dark apricot sky. All the despair I've kept trapped in my chest pushes against my ribs, my heart a rotating red planet with its own gravity drawing me forward.

e.g., Shaking, I pull out my phone and tap his number. He answers on the third ring.

"Hey, kiddo," he says.

His voice envelops me, familiar and sweet, one of the first voices I have ever known. Tears run down my cheeks.

"Hi, Daddio," I say.

"How's my only daughter?"

What would you do if you knew it was the last time? Because I know it will be the last time. A sob escapes my throat.

"What's wrong, honey? Are those fuckers fucking with you again?"

"Not anymore, no," I say.

"Then what's got you crying?"

"Just homesick, is all."

"What's she saying?" my mother shrieks in the background. "Is she okay? She's never okay! Is she crying again?"

"Ah, well, there's nothing here for you, remember? You've got your new fancy life out there."

Nothing here for you. The moments with him that I've crystallized within me rise to the surface: him reading the newspaper to me in the kitchen while I ate cereal as a little girl, teaching me to drive, taking me to the art museums, introducing me to books, waving as my train left for college, the phone calls, his wisdom, his gray hair and sparkling blue eyes, his temper, his great heart.

"I was thinking of you," I say. "I wanted you and Mom to know that I miss you and I love you."

"I love you, too, honey bun. Now, stop that damn crying. You know how I hate mushy shit. Be safe, okay?"

I crystallize the sound of his voice. I put it in the glass jar of my heart. The line goes dead. *Anything that can happen will happen.*

e.g., The sweet scent of the black hole envelops me, all metal, flesh, fruit. It begins to spin and hum, then it sings my name, holding the dark note grandly, as if it is the final scene of a long opera.

The red of a pomegranate rises up within me, a new madness, fresh and wild, the colors of San Francisco suddenly bright despite the smoke, the edges of buildings sharp as knives, the cold air burning my throat, my life replaying itself as if on a flickering screen: California, the chef, the CEO, the city, Sasha, the man on fire, the men split open on the train tracks, the man beneath my window howling, howling, howling, all of his pain in his howl, the suffering in the world in his howl, all the want of my life, everything I chased only to find nothing, the clinic, *she's just going to let the air in*, the city on fire, the protests, the virus crawling through the air, infecting the city one by one, some of us to live on, to live on here, on this earth, as if it were some kind of prize, as if we were lucky. I see my father, my mother, my brother, in a place where I can't return because I'm someone else, my face is no longer the same, *anything that can happen will happen*, they wouldn't even recognize me. All the bittersweet horror and beauty of life crashes down on me.

The black hole draws closer, ever closer, the darkness blotting out the old world, offering another future, another path, offering either an ending or a beginning.

I step forward. For once, I do not waver. I look up into the familiar darkness. With the red fruit of my heart full in my throat, I give myself up.

Acknowledgments

This novel would not exist without the endless support of my family. My deepest thanks go to Kent D. Wolf and Emily Polson for their belief in this project and hard work bringing it to life. In addition, I'm grateful to: Tommy Pico, Laura van den Berg, Kristen Arnett, Amelia Gray, Nadia Chaudhury, Susan Johnson, Katie Reing, Missy Meyers, Demian Fenton, Don Argott, Layne and Orchid Cugini, Sam Glatt, Marci Lawson, Matt Bell, Carmen Maria Machado, Brandon Taylor, Elisa Gabbert, Rachel Yoder, Sophie Mackintosh, Emily Austin, Erin Somers, Brian Evenson, Samantha Irby, The Slacc, Katya Apekina, Kate Durbin, Jasmine Lake, and Eric and Eliza at Two Dollar Radio.

Thank you as well to the teams at NEON Literary, Scribner, and UTA.

Selected Bibliography

The definitions in this novel were compiled from multiple dictionaries and sources, including *Merriam-Webster*, *New Oxford American*, dictionary.com, and Wikipedia.

References to *Hills Like White Elephants* by Ernest Hemingway are made on pages 258–59. The line "I am a riddle in nine syllables" on page 259 is from Sylvia Plath's poem "Metaphors."

The following works helped portray the black hole in this novel:

Gubser, Steven. *The Little Book of Black Holes*. Princeton, NJ: Princeton University Press, 2017.

Hawking, Stephen. *Black Holes and Baby Universes and Other Essays*. New York: Bantam, 2017.

———. *A Brief History of Time: From the Big Bang to Black Holes*. New York: Bantam, 1988.

Lea, Robert. "Wormholes Could Explain What Happens to Matter Swallowed by a Black Hole." *Newsweek*, March 9, 2022.

Levin, Janna. *Black Hole Survival Guide*. New York: Knopf, 2020.

———. *Black Hole Blues and Other Songs from Outer Space*. New York: Anchor, 2016.

Musser, George. "The Most Famous Paradox in Physics Nears its End." *Quanta Magazine*, October 29, 2020: https://www.quantamagazine.org/the-most-famous-paradox-in-physics-nears-its-end-20201029/.

O'Neill, Ian. "Black Holes Were Such an Extreme Concept, Even Einstein Had His Doubts." History.com, April 15, 2019: www.history.com/news/black-holes-albert-einstein-theory-relativity-space-time.

Overbye, Dennis. "John A. Wheeler, Physicist Who Coined the Term 'Black Hole,' Is Dead at 96." *New York Times*, April 14, 2008: https://www.nytimes.com/2008/04/14/science/14wheeler.html#:~:text=April%2014%2C%202008-,John%20A.,Hightstown%2C%20N.J.%20He%20was%2096.

Russell, Peter. "Hawking at Harvard." *The Harvard Gazette*, April 18, 2006: https://news.harvard.edu/gazette/story/2016/04/hawking-at-harvard/.

RIPE

Sarah Rose Etter

This reading group guide for RIPE *includes an introduction, discussion questions, and ideas for enhancing your book club. The suggested questions are intended to help your reading group find new and interesting angles and topics for your discussion. We hope that these ideas will enrich your conversation and increase your enjoyment of the book.*

Introduction

Cassie is burned-out, sleep-deprived, possibly pregnant, and struggling to stay afloat at the well-funded Silicon Valley start-up she crossed the country to work for. She powers through with cold brew, cocaine, and the occasional call home to her loving but brusque father. All the while, she is accompanied by a miniature black hole that has been with her since birth. The black hole reacts to Cassie's mental state, and as she begins to doubt everything she has worked toward, the embodiment of her anxiety and depression threatens to consume her. With razor-sharp social commentary, *Ripe* tells the story of one woman's unraveling in the face of the pressure cooker that is our late-capitalist society.

Topics & Questions for Discussion

1. The novel is divided into sections based on the structure of a pomegranate: exocarp, mesocarp, membrane, and seed. Why do you think Etter organized the novel in this way? How do these terms relate to the sections they represent?

2. Talk about the "Believers" and how they function within the novel. According to Cassie, "Believers" are people who "were born to be" in Silicon Valley and "come from the Ivy League and throw their entire beings into technology" (page 6). What do you make of this class of people Cassie describes?

3. In order to keep up when life is too demanding, Cassie divides herself into her "true self" and her "false self." She often lets her false self take over to handle a presentation, a coworker, or catty acquaintances. What do you think about Cassie's method of splitting herself into two in this way? What does it say about how she views herself?

4. To create a stronger sense of camaraderie, Sasha, a co-founder of VOYAGER, has Cassie and her coworkers divulge their most traumatic experiences to one another. This

backfires for Cassie, who then feels actively antagonistic toward the group. How else does this "forced intimacy" come up in the novel? Does Cassie have genuine relationships with any of her coworkers? What about her friends?

5. Throughout the novel, Etter juxtaposes scenes of disturbing violence with Cassie's mundane yet toxic workplace environment (a man self-immolates on her way home from work, she witnesses a crow devouring a duckling outside her office window, her train is delayed after a work event due to someone jumping onto the tracks, and so on). How do these scenes set the tone of the novel? How does living with this contrast affect Cassie?

6. Discuss the way that Etter blends scientific research into the novel. What effect does she achieve by interspersing Cassie's "Notes & Research" about black holes into the timeline of the story?

7. Consider the black hole that accompanies Cassie. Though its presence mostly baffles her, there are times she describes it as being protective. How does the black hole contribute to your understanding of Cassie? Of the events of the novel? Do you think the black hole has a physical presence or is it all in Cassie's head? How does your experience of the novel change with each interpretation?

8. "When I was young, I thought God was a giant eye in the sky, spying on the world below" (page 209). Cassie serves as both the watched and the watcher at different points in

the story. What role does being observed or observing play in the novel? What does this suggest about the nature of surveillance or self-surveillance?

9. What role does love play in the novel, if any? Cassie offers a few versions of love when describing her relationship with her family members. "My mother stung and stung . . ." Cassie says. "Some part of love must be the stinging" (page 15). But about her brother, she says, "I loved him in that silent way, the way where you don't even have to talk about it" (page 62). How do we see Cassie's understanding of love manifest? What impact does it have on her romantic relationship?

10. Cassie experiences a series of personal crises over the course of the novel, but the book is also set against the backdrop of several global ones—raging wildfires, soaring rates of unhoused people, and a rapidly spreading virus. How did these catastrophes influence Cassie's personal journey and mental health? What parts of her experiences remind you of your own, whether in the early days of 2020 or today?

11. The novel is ripe with pomegranate imagery and metaphors. Why do you think Etter chose this particular fruit? How is this symbol working in the novel?

12. Discuss your interpretation of the ending of *Ripe*. What did you make of Cassie's decision-making leading up to this point? What is your ultimate takeaway after the events of the novel?

Enhance Your Book Club

1. Museums hold a certain importance for Cassie and serve as a place of self-reflection in the novel. Visit a local history or art museum by yourself and meditate on the experience.

2. Take a look at the works listed in the Selected Biography and consider reading some of them to supplement your understanding of black holes.

3. Read Sarah Rose Etter's previous novel, *The Book of X*— whose protagonist is also named Cassie—and discuss the thematic crossover between the books. Do you think there is a connection between them?

Reading group guide written by Sabrina Pyun

A Conversation with
Sarah Rose Etter

Emily Polson (editor of *Ripe*): What's the origin story of this novel?

Sarah Rose Etter: The first line came to me—"A man shouldn't be seen like that, all lit up"—while I was living in San Francisco. I worked at a Silicon Valley start-up for a year, and I was struck by the disparity between the wealthy and the unhoused. I commuted to Silicon Valley by train from the Mission, roughly three hours round-trip.

Every day, I just saw so much suffering existing alongside so much money. A coffee shop owner told me she'd seen a man set himself on fire outside of the shop and had tried to put him out. That story stuck with me—it was so gruesome that I couldn't shake it.

Throughout my time in Silicon Valley, I took notes on what everyone around me was going through—our days, our parties, the increasing tension and rent, the way tech people interacted with the unhoused. I had expected California to be golden, glistening, incredible—and instead I found a city eroding, stores shuttering, the strange feeling that everything was wrong.

I called my father at home back east constantly to get advice.

I was exhausted, depressed, confused, lonely. And he always answered. At the end of almost every phone call, he would say: *Write this all down. You're going to make this a novel one day and sell a million copies.*

I was also reading frequently on the train: Joan Didion's *Play It as It Lays*, Shirley Jackson's *The Bird's Nest*, Anna Wiener's *Uncanny Valley*, Anne Carson's *Nox*. I took something different from each one of those books—the use of language, the sentence structure, the POV—when writing *Ripe*.

A few months before lockdown, my father died suddenly of a heart attack. So in my grief and isolation, I wrote this book for him, the book he always wanted me to write.

EP: Is that where the idea for the black hole came from? Some of the scenes in the book, when Cassie's alone in her apartment with the black hole growing larger and larger above her, threatening to consume her . . . I can imagine that's what being alone with your grief felt like during those months of sheltering in place.

SRE: Absolutely. This is a harder part of the novel for me to talk about, but while I was deep in this grief and isolation, I was entirely lost. I had been through a lot of pain in my life, but this pain was so searing, it was almost exquisite yet unbearable. I was consumed with wanting to be wherever my father was—but in this case, he was dead. I felt like one of those young animals in a nature show who keeps looking for their parent who has been shot and killed. I just kept thinking: *But where did he go?*

The black hole was a product of that—I couldn't understand life without him and I was trying to figure that out. It also mirrored my grief—it was endless, an abyss, it kept changing shape. On certain days I could pull myself out of it, and on other days, I had to let myself be sucked into it entirely. The black hole for Cassie is certainly depression—but for me, it was a way to understand grief and mortality.

EP: I like that it can be read as a literal black hole—a surreal element—but also works as a metaphor. I related a lot to Cassie's internal struggles—the black hole was like a key to unlocking language I didn't have to describe those dark nights of the soul as well as the tender moments of love and desire that help us survive them. But I'm also quick to describe *Ripe*, perhaps blithely, as a "sad girl book." Critics have done the same—*NYLON* called you a "prophet for the sad girls," and the *New York Times Book Review* references the "long history of sad girls and women in literature" in their review of *Ripe*, evoking Joan Didion, Sylvia Plath. How do you feel about this label?

SRE: I try really hard not to get hung up on labels because I do think they are a function of capitalism. Most artists don't sit down and say, "I'm going to write a feminist book!"—these are words we apply to the work after the fact so we can place it, understand it, put it on the right shelf. With "sad girl lit," I just sort of accepted it as the shorthand for books that are selling well right now and are part of a trend. But that lineage goes back to Didion and Plath and lots of other writers who just happen to not be men. Obviously, being put into a category with these greats doesn't bother me—that's incredible company. But all literature is sad, and men have been writing their sad bullshit for decades and we don't call it "sad boy lit."

EP: Right. Let's start referring to Hemingway and Fitzgerald as part of "the long history of sad boys and men in literature" and see if it catches on. I mentioned surrealism, but the science was another thing that really drew me to your work. Part of what's so fascinating about black holes is how even physicists' speculation about them enters the realm of science fiction—the very real possibility that wormholes exist, for example. When I started editing this book, I watched the documentary *Black Holes: The Edge of All We Know*, and one of the interviewees said: "I think the dream of any physicist who studies black holes is to be able to go through the horizon and to the other side. If I could take this trip, having decided that I've had enough of this world, what would I see?" What kind of research did you do on black holes, and how did it impact the way the black hole took shape over the course of your writing process? How did you approach arranging the Notes & Research sections for the reader?

SRE: I did extensive, extensive research on black holes—on what they are, the way we personify them through language, how they behave, what would happen if you entered one. This required reading books, news articles, research papers, and watching documentaries. I read a lot of work from Stephen Hawking, Janna Levin, and Carl Sagan. This was probably the most challenging and rewarding part of the book—figuring out how to turn this interstellar mystery into a character.

With all of my books, as I get later into the editing process, I realize I want to give the reader some breathing room from the emotional intensity of the narrative—sometimes, that's as simple as adding a page with a lot of white space. In *Ripe*, these pages give the work some breathing room and hopefully provide the reader with enough context to understand black holes, too. I also think those sections work as a reminder that no matter how surreal my novel might be, the world around us is just as surreal.

EP: Yes! Those pages, along with the growing black hole graphic and the pomegranate section openers, do that so well. The pomegranate is a central image of the book, and some readers have pointed out it can be read as an allusion to the myth of Persephone, but I was most fascinated by how it gives the novel structure. How did you come up with this idea?

SRE: I know this is going to sound arrogant, but my goal with every book is to write something that's never been done before—and much of that comes down to playing with form and structure. These elements are the fun part—with the pomegranate, I knew I wanted a four-part structure, and I loved the idea of going from the outside of the fruit to the inside. It guided the narrative—the first section is about Cassie's outer life, and it just goes deeper and deeper until finally we're inside her body.

Some of these structural explorations are just to keep me going as a writer—they work as my guideposts into the narrative. Sometimes, those elements get stripped out during editing—sometimes, they stay in. It is interesting to think about the book without it—without the pomegranate, the black holes, the definitions. How would that change the narrative or the reading of it? Would it be a better or worse book? I don't know.

EP: Since you mentioned it, tell me about the decision to start all of the flashback chapters with a word and its definition.

SRE: The definitions were a way for me to give the reader enough context and background to understand Cassie and her decisions. Her way of looking at the world is deeply informed by these flashes of the past that the reader needs in order to empathize with her. I was also really interested in how memory works. I aimed to have the structure of the book function so that Cassie might hear a word and have a memory triggered. Each section of the book that starts with a definition is essentially a wormhole back to her roots—and is meant to replicate what happens when a memory suddenly comes back to you. So, I looked into how the human mind operates—and how and why we remember. I wanted to create that sensation where you smell someone's cologne and remember your first high school boyfriend, that deep sensory memory you can never shake.

EP: Roxane Gay called this book "a master class in creating tension." How did you build suspense into a story with so much interiority?

SRE: Some of this came from films I was watching—*Parasite* and *Uncut Gems*. Both of those movies, I remember almost having a panic attack in the theater from how the stakes just kept being raised, everyone kept making the wrong decisions, it just kept getting worse in ways you couldn't predict. Those experiences really drove this idea of constant escalation throughout the novel. I know some readers might hate that or be turned off by it. But I do genuinely think the worst thing a work of art can do is make people feel nothing. I would rather give you a panic attack than bore you to the point where you drop the book five pages in and never come back to it.

EP: I loved *Parasite* but got so stressed within the first five minutes of *Uncut Gems* I couldn't finish it! But I raced through your manuscript because I needed to know how you were going to release all the built-up tension. No spoilers, but the first time I read the ending, I threw my e-reader across the room. Then I picked it up, went back to the beginning, and reread until I'd come up with a more hopeful way to interpret the final scene. This was something we talked a lot about during the editing process, so I'm curious—how have readers responded to the ending? Do you hope they interpret it in a particular way?

SRE: I get a lot of questions about this in my DMs, but I'm far less interested in my interpretation of the ending than what the reader takes from it. It's sort of like a surreal painting, right? Yes, the artist placed a series of objects on the canvas, but ultimately, it is the viewer's subconscious response to the work that matters. To me, it really does come down to where science has most recently landed—the dichotomy presented in the final Notes & Research section. My reading of that can change depending on the day, whether I'm feeling bleak and lost, or hopeful and kind.

EP: That's been my favorite thing to ask people after they've read the book—I recently visited family, and my mom, sister, and aunt all had different takes on it. My other favorite reader reaction was someone who said it made them want to quit their job, and I think it's made a lot of us reevaluate our relationship with hustle culture and the performance of productivity. How are you getting along with the capitalist machine these days, and how do you balance your full-time job with your writing career?

SRE: I don't think you and I have had a chance to talk much about this—because the last time I saw you, I was on book tour and we were both really caught up in that whirlwind together. But it has been very strange to have this book come out, and have it really take over my entire life for so many months and years, and then just go back to work. It feels almost like the book happened to someone else.

But on the plus side, I do think my day job stops me from falling into the ego pit that can come with publishing a book. You can't get too caught up in the reviews or the press—not that I don't appreciate and love those things, because I do, so much. This has been a dream, all the way through. Having the job, though, does keep my feet on the ground in a very real way.

In terms of balance, I haven't really nailed it. It depends on the stage of the process—if I'm just at home writing drafts, that's easier than when I'm on the press tour. I am also lucky to have bosses and a company that really support me doing this work—we have unlimited paid vacation time, so I was able to take off every Friday for a month so I could do all of my interviews for the book on those days, instead of code-switching between that and work meetings all day.

That said, after so many months of work with you and everyone at Scribner leading up to publication, I really am in resting mode right now, and that feels beautiful. I'm just reading and spending time with my dog and doing my job. So I guess that's a form of balance—going all in when you need to, but making up for it afterward.

EP: Speaking of reading for fun, your manuscript reminded me of other great novels about work and tech culture—*Self Care*

by Leigh Stein, *Temporary* by Hilary Leichter, *The Startup Wife* by Tahmima Anam—and after we started working on *Ripe* together, I read several others, which you mentioned earlier, that resonated at your recommendation. What other books and media do you hope *Ripe* is in conversation with? Any deep cuts you want to recommend to readers who love your work and want to dive further into your influences?

SRE: You know, I think I'm a bit of a freak—I try to avoid reading books that are about what I'm writing about. It's way too easy for me to get wrapped up in what the other author is doing and lose track of my own voice. It can also give me this feeling of "Oh, someone already did this, who needs another novel about work?"

Obviously, all of the writers you mention are insanely talented—Hilary is such a dear friend and I love *Temporary*! But I really tried to read those books after the first draft was done. Mostly, I was going back to these sort of stripped-down novels about people experiencing the world—Joy Williams's *The Changeling*, Deborah Levy's *Hot Milk*. I also read a lot of Barbara Comyns—*The Vet's Daughter* was a big one. But I'm also really big on literature in translation, so there were some others—Tove Ditlevsen's *The Copenhagen Trilogy*, Fernanda Melchor's *Hurricane Season*, Marieke Lucas Rijneveld's *The Discomfort of Evening*, Aglaja Veteranyi's *Why the Child Is Cooking in the Polenta*.

Sometimes, when I needed a break, I would pick up the *New Yorker* to read the nonfiction, which is sometimes the most generative for me. I also tossed some graphic novels into the mix—*Black Hole* and *Last Look* by Charles Burns. There are also two great books by Mason Currey called *Daily Rituals*—one is specifically about women artists. Those two books just list out the routines of great writers and artists, and it motivated me to see how other people kept going every day and finished the work.

EP: Last question. In *Ripe*, Cassie's father tells her: "Life is a series of big moments. Some days, of course, you're out there digging ditches. Some days, it's just a Tuesday, you know? But then there are the big moments. And you have to save them in your heart, crystallize them, and put them in a glass jar." What's one big moment from your experience of writing and publishing *Ripe* that lives in a glass jar in your heart?

SRE: I've gotten this question a lot actually—but it's hard, because publishing a novel is a long process. It never felt like there was one BIG moment—it felt like so many incredible moments—but there are a few I will always remember: the *New York Times* review coming out on this random Sunday and bursting into tears; seeing you that night at Franklin Park to kick off the book tour when we both just teared up after so much work we had done together was paying off; walking out with Roxane for the event at the Strand and seeing all of my friends and family in the crowd, including my father's brother, my uncle Tom, and just seeing him with tears in his eyes.

But then, too, there was a moment much earlier—and it was the first time you and I spoke on the phone, when you were interested in *Ripe*. Your questions and thoughts about the book were so spot-on—and you weren't trying to turn it into a happy book or force the shape of it into something else. And I remember having this sort of dazed but sure feeling that you were going to be my editor, and it really was a beautiful moment.

EP: That was such a singular experience for me, too. It was my first-ever author call for a book I wanted to acquire, and I was so nervous, but I remember starting off by just spewing a bunch of things I loved about the book, and we clicked immediately. That's what made walking out into the rare book room at the Strand on the night of your launch event so memorable for me—we started off with just the two of us on a call, and a year and a half later we were done, and over a hundred people had gathered in this beautiful space filled with strings of lights to support you and celebrate this wonderful achievement. I remember you saying later that this must be how people feel walking down the aisle on their wedding day.

SRE: You read my mind. I can still tear up thinking about that moment—so it must be the one crystallized in the glass jar of my heart.